KARSTEN KREPINSKY

Berlin 2039

Translated from the German by
KARIN DUFNER

First published with the title *Berlin 2039 – Der Tod nimmt alle mit* in 2016 by Karsten Krepinsky/Neuwelt Verlag.
Cover design by Ingo Krepinsky, Die TYPONAUTEN
www.typonauten.de/eng
Printed and published by BoD – Books on Demand, Norderstedt
ISBN: 9783753439402

www.theworldbehindthewindow.com

About the Book

Berlin 2039 – The Reign Of Anarchy

Population has doubled within the last twenty years, leading to a living hell where poverty, crime, and claustrophobia rule. Those who can afford it, have withdrawn to the well-protected gated communities, while the police have left entire neighborhoods to their own devices. In these lawless blank spots, the authorities use so-called pushers to maintain a level of constant unrest between Arab clans, Turkish gangs, and Chechen brotherhoods. They are mavericks, men and women outside the law, who only answer to their supervisors based in the LKA, which is short for *Landeskriminalamt*, the State Office of Criminal Investigation. This is the story of Hauke the Pusher and Detective Natasha…

Dedicated to the freedom of thought

Berlin Locations:

Prenzlauer Berg
Today: a white middle and upper class neighborhood
2039: now **P'berg**, a gated community behind barbed wire, seemingly a safe haven for civil servants and government officials

Kreuzberg
Today: a bohemian neighborhood, inhabited by students, hipsters, and immigrants with touches of gentrification
2039: now **X'berg**, a place with a great view of the Ghetto where bored young "Globals" live in expensive penthouses

Friedrichshain
Today: a bohemian neighborhood with a lively nightclub scene
2039: now **F'hain**, dubbed The Ghetto.

Wedding
Today: a working class and immigrant neighborhood with a few students tossed in the mix
2039: the puffer zone between the rich and the poor population

Wannsee
Today: a very upscale neighborhood
2039: ditto

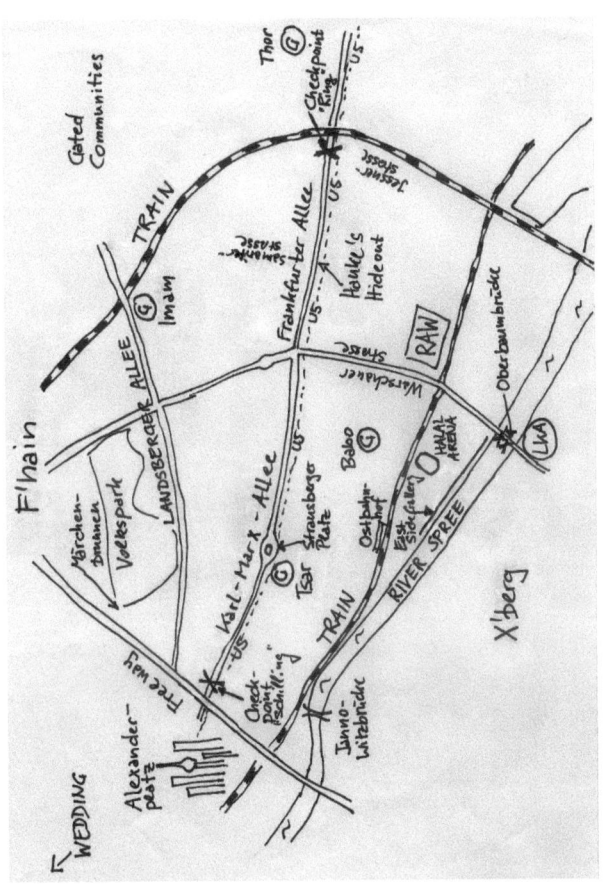

"We won't stand idly by while this human trash gnaws its way through the city of Berlin like a cancerous growth. Therefore, I have given order to immediately seal off those areas of the city forever lost to us..."

From the press statement of Chancellor Vasily Schmidt on the *National Emergency Act* of August 23, 2036.

Three years later...

Prologue

The dead man's cap has come off, his white caftan is soaked with blood. Slumped forward on a chair, his head lies on the kitchen table in a pool of blood. The skull has been smashed, more blood is oozing from a deep wound. Remains of his last meal cling to his full beard. The killer wipes his cudgel on his victim's robe, kisses the wooden crucifix he is wearing around his neck on a leather thong, and pulls his hood down deeper into his face. He is an apparition, dressed in worn-out shabby clothes. All in gray and covered in the dirt of the streets. His face hidden in the half-shadow of his hood, he pulls a playing card from a fabric pouch secured with a length of rope and crams it between the murdered man's index and middle fingers. He sits down next to him at the table, pulls the soup plate closer, tears off a piece of pita bread, dunks it into the soup, and starts eating. Rivulets of arterial blood mingle with meat broth. The killer reaches for the glass of black tea, empties it, gets up, and places plate and glass in the sink, which he then stops up and opens the faucet. With a wordless nod he takes one last look at the dead Salafist, as if a score had just been settled. Before he leaves the kitchen, he turns off the light.

1

The *Lemons* call all Germans potatoes. Or Jews, if they happen to be in a bad mood. Which they usually are. Especially because F'hain is surrounded by a fence with checkpoints now, effectively blocking their access to the better-off citizens of Berlin. Concrete steles and soldiers, sporting assault rifles. MG nests, sheltered behind walls of sandbags. Those obstacles can really be a challenge, even for a testosterone-controlled kid of the Ghetto. Barriers and checkups remind me of the Holy Land somehow, if you know what I mean. In some places the fence is already being replaced with a wall. An installation that seems to be meant for eternity. Thus, leaving F'hain has become difficult. The high-rises of Alexanderplatz, the posh shopping malls of Potsdamer Platz, or the fancy boutiques of Friedrichstrasse are now out of reach for most people here. And the future doesn't look rosy. Now and then I can see those poor devils at their windows. The losers of this world, you know what I mean. With all their dreams of happiness and wealth. Them, who spend their evenings standing at the drafty windows of the run-down dumps they live in, because all the violence around stops them from venturing out in the streets. Pasty faces pressed against the glass and eyes filled with yearning, they gaze into the far distance. They breathe the same air as the *Globals* at Alexanderplatz. They look up to the same sky. But fate has dumped them on the wrong side of the fence. Once Ghetto, always Ghetto.

Once upon a time we had another wall in Berlin—this was fifty years ago. Almost ten years before I was born. Nobody knows about it anymore, because in the Ghetto book-learning doesn't mean shit. The Quran is the only book that counts. In many areas of F'hain life is ruled by Sharia, Islamic law. The version favored by the *Imam*, that is. The Quran leaves lots of room for interpretation, you'd better take my word for it, my friends. Even the *Lemons* themselves constantly bicker about it. Other than the big-shots living in the Wannsee neighborhood would like to believe, they don't form a monolithic bloc. Far from it: the Turks hate the Arabs, the Kurds hate the Turks, and everyone hates the Chechens. And the Arabs? Who cares who the Arabs hate? I also have no idea why the Muslims are called *Lemons*. Maybe because of their typically dour faces, as if they'd just bitten down on a lemon. Don't get me wrong. Germans or Muslims, it doesn't mean a thing to me. I don't even look like an Aryan myself. An ex-girlfriend once told me that my features were those of a generic immigrant. Mediterranean type, anything from Turk to Arab, a light-skinned one, that is. Maybe that's why they picked me for this job. Because, with my dark hair and my Middle-Eastern complexion I almost pass as a *Lemon*.

I'm not ashamed to say that there also might be a little Jewish blood flowing in my veins. My swarthy looks have to come from somewhere, right? As cute as the idea might sound, it's not very likely that my great-great-grandmother succumbed to the charms of an Italian migrant laborer, working at the railway tracks in early nineteenth-century Germany. You all know how people tend to romanticize their family backgrounds. Every Tom, Dick, and Harry likes to think of himself as the heir to some blue-blooded name. No, I'm serious. I'm convinced that there must be some Semitic influence. Just regular Jewish blood, coursing through my body. Even though my eyes are blue. That's something that means a lot to me. I don't need to resort to colored contact lenses like many Lemons are doing it now. Some of these jokers even dye their hair blond. I guess they hope that it will further their careers. But it's not easy to get the Ghetto out of your system.

One more thing you need to know about me is, that I'm no fan of organized religion. Opium for the masses, that's what it is to me. And, God knows, I'm not alone with this view. Plus, I also prefer to be in charge of my own drug supply. I work as a Pusher for the LKA and my job is to adjust the "balance of power" in the neighborhood. This involves evening the scales between the different Godfathers by making sure that the bosses will continue their war against each other: the *Tsar*, the *Imam*, the *Babo*, and the *Emperor*. If one of them shows signs of getting too much ahead in the game, he needs to be cut down a notch to prevent violence from spilling over Ghetto limits. Human trash is supposed to fight among themselves, right? As the LKA doesn't like to get their hands dirty they use drug dealers like us. Off the record, of course. When one of the Godfathers gains too much power, it's our job to give the competition a leg-up with the help of well-placed donations. As you can probably guess pushers aren't the most popular of people. When we supply his competitors with merchandise, the *Imam* is sure to hear about it. Still, this system works remarkably well. In the realm of organized crime bosses tend to think like politicians. They, too, form new alliances every day. And an offer of friendship that comes in the guise of a suitcase full of free drugs often has a healing effect.

My name is Hauke, by the way. The nuns in the Catholic orphanage who raised me were great fans of the novel *The*

Dykemaster by Theodor Storm. Maybe you've heard of the story about the mad dike warden, who's my namesake. And my background? Does it really make a difference? They plucked me from a baby flap at Urban Hospital, that's what I always claim, at least. Dropped off anonymously. Family unknown. Not an ounce of blue blood, this much can be assumed. And surely no Baby Moses. If you could see me now, odds are that you wouldn't take me for the toughest guy in the 'hood. Rather the opposite. I'm clean shaven and neat, wear a black suit, and even carry a briefcase at all times to look respectable. Stuffed with dope, of course. It's also equipped with a hidden compartment with an Uzi in it for self-defense, an absolute must-have. I also pack a Glock 17 in a shoulder holster. One of the best handguns I know. Reliable and precise. Nineteen rounds. My special trick is to always load it up with a rubber round first. Underneath, there is a regular 9mm cartridge, followed by a dum-dum bullet that will burst open upon impact, virtually shredding the opponent to bits. I call this my three steps of escalation. Step one: the warning. Step two: the chastisement. Step three? Game over, player one. Not a beautiful thing to behold, I can tell you. I'm not a gun-toting weapons fanatic, I swear. And not one of these army types either who give their rifles names. I also don't like using my fists. I never once had my nose broken. It's something to be proud of, I tell you.

Things just don't seem to improve. Not in the Ghetto. Once you've reached your early forties, you start seeing things clearer while abandoning your illusions. Just the other day I was held up by a little kid. Maybe eight years old, I guess. The tyke pointed a knife at my crotch and demanded my money. When I explained that I only had dope, he happily toddled off with five units of coke. What can I tell you? It can get a little trying to adhere to one's principles out here. Human values and such. At least I've managed to remain one of the few Pushers who don't sample their own merchandise. Okay, I pop psycho meds. But only those which need a prescription. So don't get any wrong ideas. Plus, I went off these pills a while ago, because I want to be myself again. The name of the stuff, I'm using? None of your business, I think. We don't know each other that well yet. But, hey, things can always change. Follow me or leave me alone. It's the same to me. But there's one thing I promise you: I won't lie. This is something you can count on.

2

Natasha sounded rather worried on the phone. Have I told you about her yet? She's my supervisor at the LKA. She coordinates my jobs with me, procures the drugs, and informs me of the latest developments. The LKA has just moved into new headquarters in X'berg across the river. To the spot where the *Watergate* used to be, if you happen to remember this club. Electronic music on two floors, adjacent to Oberbaumbrücke. This was a lifetime ago. Now, the investigators have a perfect view of the Ghetto from their brand new glass-enclosed high-rise. Maybe they use their roof antennas to listen in on the junkies' chattering. They might also be watching the traffic of losers on the streets. Or they're eavesdropping on the constant squabbling among the ultra-orthodox Muslims, while barely able to stifle a yawn.

Natasha. She's different. A special person, a trait I noticed at once. Not one of these beauties who're only good as clothes-horses. She also has a good head on her shoulders. And personality. A first-class lady. Well bred. From a good family, I think. Even though I never ask. Certain things are better left to imagination. She's not married, I believe. But she also might just not be wearing a ring around the Ghetto. There's a boyfriend now and then, I guess. No one on a permanent basis.

I'm driving down Frankfurter Allee in my Lincoln Continental. A real classic car that guzzles up more than ten gallons per one hundred miles. That's a lousy gas-mileage, I can hear you say. But who the fuck cares? In F'hain nobody goes long distances anyway. The Ghetto isn't all that large. It's all a matter of being seen.

Natasha wants to meet at RAW, the ancient train depot bearing the name "Reichsbahnausbesserungswerk" that was transformed into a cultural center a long time ago. Its compound is located on Warschauer Strasse, a boulevard lined with dead plane trees that everyone started to call "The Warsaw" last year. This name-change is related to an incident in the fall, when a Chechen decided to chop a biker into two halves with a chain saw. A dramatic event, even in the Ghetto. The bloodstains on the tarmac were only covered up with sawdust. Thus, the traces of this gruesome act of violence remained in plain view until a week later, when it finally rained again. Usually, the Chechens don't tend to do things in halves—pardon my pun. Their signature is to skin their victims, a habit they picked up during the Afghan war in the eighties, when Grandpa Chechen fought against the Mujaheddin side by side with the Red Army. This was when there still was a Soviet Union. Damn. Does this odd construction of states still ring anyone's bell? Probably for the Communists among you. However, I find it vital to know one's history, as you must have realized by now. Looking into the past to put the future into perspective. It shows me what we are and what will become of us. Anyway, two years ago the Chechens had the brilliant idea to skin the boss of the Arab clan and to display his body right next to the Märchenbrunnen, the fairy-tale fountain, in Volkspark. The Grimm Brothers' bedtime stories taken to the extreme. Had they only known who was going to follow the impaled ruler to the throne, as in this case they might have preferred to instead share a pipe of peace. Because Ali Bansuri, the new *Imam*, retaliated by beheading six Chechens with his own hand. There are rumors around that he still keeps their heads somewhere in his mosque. The result was some back-and-forth traffic that went on for a while. Friendly visits on one, declarations of love on the other side. In the end, a good four hundred people were dead and power structures had been restored to normal. A field day for pushers, I can tell you. I just had to comfortably lean back with a cold beer and watch the activities unfold. But no more reminiscing. You don't get a new *Imam* every day. Now, the conflict has to be carefully rekindled. The flickering flame needs to be fanned.

In the Warsaw the new *Imam's* word is law, just like that of his predecessor. All the way from RAW up to the former stockyard, today the site of his humongous mosque. The area north of the old Ostbahnhof, the eastern train station, is controlled by Selim, called the *Babo*. And around Strausberger Platz the *Tsar*, this wily Chechen bandit, is pulling the strings. The bikers of Aryan Motorcircle with their president Thor, dubbed the *Emperor* by the *Lemons*, are at the bottom of the food chain. The *Emperor's* realm is limited to a narrow strip of land in the east around Jessnerstrasse. He also is the only one of the bosses who resides outside the Ghetto in the former Stasi headquarters in Ruschestrasse. Stasi? Does it ring a bell? For those of you who were too zoned out during history class in school: it's short for "Staatssicherheitsdienst," the former Eastern Germany's secret service. The *Emperor* carries a lot of clout in Lichtenberg, which isn't part of the Ghetto. Thor's time in F'hain, however, seems to be up. Therefore, regular deliveries to him by yours truly wouldn't make much sense. He doesn't have many minions left anyhow, as the number of native Germans around here is dwindling, most of them having moved to the borough of Wedding. The only ones remaining are the seniors, the indigents, a few Christian missionaries, the junkies, and the hookers. You might think that a Christian missionary's life expectancy must be pretty short in an out and out Muslim 'hood. But owing to one of the many enigmatic ways of life, these religious zealots usually are left alone. Chances to die a martyr: absolutely zilch. No idea why. Maybe the bosses don't see them as a threat. Sometimes, the logic of the street is a mystery even to me. But facts are facts. And a fact goes without explaining, as it has a life of its own.

I was lying about the Lincoln, by the way. Well, I do own the car, but the wheels have been removed and the engine has been stolen. I haven't been able to drive it for a long time. I can't even sit in it anymore, because someone has taken a shit on the seat. Pardon my French, but I can't think of a better word to describe this atrocity. Possessions aren't worth the trouble around here anyway. Things are changing owners much too fast. Property is hugely overestimated. I just take what I need and leave it behind when it's no longer of service. I wouldn't exactly call it Communism. Anarchic anti-collectivism would be more like it. Roaming the neighbor-hood on foot makes more sense anyhow. This way I can pass a baggie here and drop off a pouch there. Do some street-socializing. And always give to the homeless, something I highly recommend. A unit now and then doesn't hurt anyone, and these guys will be eternally grateful.

On my walk along the Warsaw I come across a kebab store with three young *Lemons* loitering in front of it. Already from the distance I get the feeling that they're looking for trouble. These children of the gutter usually communicate in a blend of German, Arabic, English, Turkish, and Russian. The teens sport sweatpants, gold chains, and gilded watches. And the ubiquitous base caps, which have been part of the uniform for decades. The scimitars the generation before them only wore as pendants around their necks, are now dangling from their belts, ready for action. On my approach I listen in on their conversation—or whatever you want to call their staccato-like grunts.

"Wanna go X'berg, slap rich dudes, yalla?" Shorty's just suggesting to his two companions. As if these jokers could simply take a stroll across River Spree when the mood hits them.

"Yalla" and "Hey, man, gross." His friends don't seem to be averse to a little outing. "Yalla" originally means "Let's go!". Meanwhile, the word has found an inflationary use and is good for almost everything, even as a verb. "I'll go home" in street lingo is "Me yalla home". And "Me yalla yo" stands for "I'll kill you". I think so, at least, because things turned nasty every time someone said it to me.

Shorty plants himself in my path, legs spread. "Yo, kuffar, yalla," he accuses me, the infidel. I give him credit for the fact that he doesn't know who he's messing with. Always watch out for the small guys. They often need to make up for something and are nimble fighters and also hard to shoot. He fondles his crotch. De-escalation is useless with dudes like him. They only chalk it off to weakness. Therefore, I resort to my standard program. "Anything interesting to discover down there?"

"*Deez-cov-er?*" Shorty repeats. The word obviously isn't part of his vocabulary.

"Because you seem to have trouble finding it," I reply, pointing at his crotch.

"Yalla! Sonofabitch, yalla." Shorty is clearly not amused. Self-irony, my friends, is something gang bangers are sadly lacking in.

"Show de fucker, Jihad," one of his comrades edges him on.

I haven't mentioned it yet, but my briefcase happens to be rigged. If you want to survive in the Ghetto, it's advisable to have a couple of tricks up your sleeve. The lower edge of my briefcase is equipped with a telescopic needle, which I can release by pressing a button underneath the handle. A little nudge with the case, just in passing and hardly noticeable, and the fine needle shoots out, pierces the flesh, and injects half a milliliter of neurotoxin into the opponent's bloodstream. This is the treatment Jihad gets, who's still blocking my way. The thug's leg immediately turns numb, making him drop to the ground.

"Yalla, sonofabitch, I fuck yo and yo family, yalla." He's a little confused and tries to get his head around what has just happened to him. Still, he continues to list the members of my extended family he plans to bring to bodily harm and keeps on spouting abuse, all the while feverishly rubbing his paralyzed leg. I pull my Glock and release a rubber round that hits home smack in the middle of his forehead. Blissful quiet settles over the scene, at last. His friends scurry into the kebab store. Respect is something money can't buy. You have to earn it. I keep on walking without looking back. If they try to cause me any more trouble, it'll be time for escalation step two.

Natasha is waiting for me at the entrance of RAW. I throw her a quick, suggestive look. Inside of me, a mad longing rears its head, but I don't give in to my urges. Sometimes you have to bid your time, it only hones the desire. But it isn't easy. I have the impression that she wouldn't mind either, because she runs her hand through her blonde hair and smiles. The SWAT guys who are with her comment our casual flirt with sneers. In the eyes of these upright civil servants I'm nothing but scum. Vermin, albeit useful sometimes. I'm not fooling myself. The tough guys have shown up in four armored Mercedes off-roaders. Balaclavas covering their faces and twitchy fingers on the triggers of their HK416s, they have taken position in the doorway where three letters rule supreme: RAW. A telltale name. Especially when I think of the sado-maso whorehouse Natasha's now taking me to. I can almost hear the question that's on the tip of your tongue: How do sado-maso practices go with Sharia? But even prostitution is *halal*—allowed—as long as the *Imam* makes a profit. The man is resourceful enough to interpret the laws of the Quran to his own liking, while keeping his people under his thumb with the help of arbitrary rules. Hell. Just like the Pope in the Vatican, the *Imam* is a questionable man of the cloth.

The Imam's Salafists, all clad in white, give me the stink eye when I enter the building with Natasha and her entourage. I'd love to hide from their hostile stares. They cover their guns with their hands, while the SWAT team walks past.

Natasha gives me a detailed description of what's awaiting me inside the whorehouse. But I'm not really listening. Like always, I'm distracted by her beauty. Maybe you know what I'm talking about. She's a sight that makes the heart of an aging Pusher beat faster. A sylphlike woman, but tough as nails. Even though I don't want to come across as being sentimental, pushers, too, can fall in love. You'd understand if you could only see her. Stroking her ponytail with her left hand, she strides along the narrow hall past the chambers that house the dominatrixes. Reddish light illuminates haphazardly stuccoed walls, where the paint is flaking off. All my attention is on Natasha. On the streets of the Ghetto unveiled women have stopped to exist, you know. The times when female *Lemons* showed at least their faces are long gone. It all started with simple headscarfs. In all variations. Slung around their heads a couple of times and secured with pins. Or loosely placed on top of their hair in granny-style. They also wore makeup, skimpy clothes, or spray-painted jeans. However, even back then there were those who hid under niqabs with only their eyes being visible. A few fans of the burka were also around. Since then poverty in the 'hood and the steady influx of people from the *Lemon* territories have drastically altered women's lives. The frivolous game, originally meant as a protest against Western values, quickly turned brutally serious. First, it was the jeans and miniskirts that vanished under dark shapeless tents. Next, makeup was gone from the faces. Until finally the faces themselves were obscured by curtains of fabric. Walking ghosts. The double-walled burka is the latest fad. I'm not joking. Should the top layer tear, there still is another one below to protect the women from prying eyes. The principle also used for double-walled oil tankers. The level of escalation can always be raised yet another notch. Times aren't getting any better, I'm telling you. Meanwhile, women affiliated with gangs and the human wrecks who have fried their brains with meth have become the only unveiled women around. The young men don't seem to mind. They just don't know any better, I guess. I, on the other hand, find it frustrating to be denied a glimpse of half-exposed tits and pert asses, when making my way through the 'hood. Freedom, my friends, is something you only learn to cherish once you've lost it. Thank God, I have a permit that allows me to get out of the Ghetto at least four times a week. Otherwise, I'd lose my mind. No idea how the *Lemons* put up with it. The only nude flesh they get to ogle is that of the girls on the billboards behind East Side Gallery. Digitalized lust on huge flat screens, about sixty feet high in the air. A free morsel, that the detested Capitalist-Christian society beyond Ghetto limits deigns to throw them. Maybe all those devout *Lemons* spend their time standing at their apartment windows and working their mangled dicks, while gawking at those hot virtual broads. Don't ask me. When the screens aren't occupied by scantily clad women bearing witness to the superiority of Western lifestyle, the watchtower staff belabors Christian catch-phrases, aimed at converting the *Lemons* to the Church of our Savior. A job cut out for Sisyphus.

"Hey, are you listening to me?" Natasha's voice eventually reaches my consciousness.

"What?" I ask, admiring her feminine curves. "Digital asses," I blurt.

Natasha laughs. "What's wrong with you? Seems like you haven't seen the inside of a whorehouse for a while."

Embarrassed, I scratch my head. "I'm a little distracted... by... I...," I stammer like an idiot.

Natasha turns and lasciviously puts her right hand on her gun in its belt holster, while tilting her body a bit to the side. I have problems meeting her eyes. She is in her thirties, but looks a lot younger. Like a ripe fruit. I should have let off some steam before this meeting. After having spent time in a Catholic boarding school the feeling that you missed out on something never seems to leave you. "What do you have for me?" I eventually ask.

"See for yourself," she replies and motions to the SWAT guy out in the hall to wait for us. Then, she leads me into a kitchen.

A dead man is slumped forward on a chair, his head resting on the table. He's white as a sheet, his limp arms dangling on left and right. His skull has been shattered. Hairs are stuck in the dark red blood that's drying on the oilcloth. The Salafist has slippers on his feet. One of it has come off. Eyes wide open, he's staring at the sink, where dishes have been left to soak. It's Yussuf Bansuri, the manager of this brothel.

"Somebody wanted to make sure," I state, when I notice the brain-matter in his hair.

"Sent to the great beyond with love. Looks like it was a matter close to someone's heart," Natasha agrees.

I just love her cynicism. A rare trait with women.

"Look at this," she points out to me.

"What?"

"Look what he's holding in his hand."

I kneel and study the dead man's hand. There's a poker card stuck between two of his fingers. Someone must have placed it there after his death, I suppose. "Ace of clubs," I announce the value of the card.

"It was the killer who wedged it between his victim's fingers," she echoes my own assumption.

I nod, yes. "A sign?"

Natasha lifts a brow, thinking. "Ever come across this symbol?"

"No."

"A gang?"

"None that I know of."

"What does it mean, you think?"

"Gambling? Gambling debts?" I joke.

She shakes her head as if I'd just said something stupid. "Stop fooling around, Hauke."

"Why are you guys here, anyway?" I ask. "I mean, since when do you care what happens inside the Ghetto?"

"The *Imam* has notified us," she explains.

"The *Imam*?" I'm surprised. "He wants the LKA involved? Why?"

"He figured that there might be trouble that couldn't be contained inside the Ghetto."

"Because of the dead manager of a whorehouse?"

"It's one of his cousins."

"So what? He'll live. Half of the Ghetto is somehow related to him."

"There seems to be more behind it. Otherwise he wouldn't have called us in," Natasha speculates.

"The Chechens?"

"I don't think so."

"Who else? The Turks?"

Natasha shakes her head, no.

"The bikers wouldn't dare pull such a stunt," I think aloud. "Thor doesn't have a death wish. It's also the Chechens he has an ax to grind with, not the Arabs. What good would it do him to raise up stink with the *Imam*?"

Natasha bends over the dead Salafist, examining the deep gash on his head. "What, do you think, did this? Baseball bat?"

"Maybe," I reply, nodding. I study her sparkling eyes. "I know what you're thinking. This simply reeks of bikers. But it doesn't mean a thing."

Natasha gives me a serious look. "The *Imam* has issued a threat against *us*."

"So?"

"If we don't hand the killer over to him, he'll declare holy war."

"So what?" I wave her off. "Why should it bother you when these jokers finish each other off?"

"Don't you understand? He wants to start a *jihad* against the infidels. The idea is to export the fight outside the ghetto."

"Out of the ghetto? What makes you think so? The ace of clubs?"

"He reads it as a Christian symbol, because the clubs are shaped like little crucifixes."

I snort. "Bullshit—it's nothing but a playing card."

"You know the *Lemons*. They wallow in the past and have successfully convinced themselves that we're the oppressors."

Natasha waves her hands. "Booooh, conspiracy, watch out," she scoffs with a tense smile. "Man, they still blame us for the crusades."

"What does Ali Bansuri think? That the LKA is behind the whole thing?"

Natasha strokes her chin. "No idea what he might be thinking." She again studies the battered man.

Same as me. "Looks pretty happy, right?" I say. "Maybe he's with his 72 virgins now."

Natasha turns around to face me. "Is everything okay with you?" she asks.

"Fine and dandy," I reply, fascinated by her luminous blue eyes and the pride reflected in them.

"You need fresh junk?" she wants to know.

I nod. "My case's almost empty."

"I brought something with me. It's outside in the car."

"Great."

"Hauke?"

"Yeah?"

"Keep your eyes open for things that might be getting out of control."

"I'll try my best."

"Lay low a little. Calm down the Arabs. Don't antagonize them."

"That'll only encourage them even more."

"The violence needs to be contained under all circumstances."

"Cheer up," I tell her. "When the going got tough last time, everything stayed inside the Ghetto."

Natasha nods pensively. "If it just wasn't for the crucifix," she says. "It's making me feel really uncomfortable."

3

I live in the subway, station Samariterstrasse. Train number 5 hasn't stopped in the Ghetto for a long time and the stations here have been closed off. But I've discovered an access to the tunnel system in a derelict building. Subways or sewers, I know my way around the city's underbelly. It's a good way to get from A to B unnoticed. As the intervals between the trains to Hauptbahnhof, the central train station, are rather short, I always have to be on the alert while walking the hundred feet or so to the abandoned platform of Samariterstrasse. From time to time police or security launch raids in the tunnels, but they leave me alone. One of the benefits of my job for the LKA is that it allows me to bribe the sheriffs with coke. I've made my home in the little ticket booth on the deserted platform, where I even have electricity and running water. Free of charge. My place is fixed up like a trailer: sleeping area, tiny kitchen, a crapper that even flushes, and a sofa. A kiosk about twenty yards away on the same platform serves me as my library, even though reading is not my only pastime down here. Every day I sit in the lounge chair I have pushed to the edge of the platform and watch the trains go by. When they slow down on approach to the station, I can make out the faces of the commuters, traveling from the boroughs of Marzahn or Hellersdorf to their jobs in Mitte, the heart of Berlin. Most of them are just dully staring ahead. But those who have window seats look at me, while I relax in my bathing shorts, my hand holding a cocktail from which I lift the little paper umbrella now and then to take a sip. Surrounded by rats and dirt. Temperatures inside the tunnel are cozy almost all year around. In the summers it can be downright humid. The working stiffs just gawk at me like at an alien. I guess to them it's like catching a glimpse of a foreign world: the thrill of the Ghetto. The situation makes it okay to take a quick look into the abyss before having to face a day at the office. I even have a couple of fans—almost exclusively female. A brunette always presses a sheet of paper to the window. "You want to marry me?" it says. Funny, how daily rituals make people eventually become parts of your life. Maybe I'll bump into her at Alexanderplatz one of these days and buy her a coffee. The thing with the rats was a bit of an exaggeration on my part, by the way. We've learned to coexist. When the occasional rodents come passing through, I usually toss them something. A piece of cheese or a bit of bread. Smart critters, they are. They learn extremely fast.

A little under three weeks ago I started sharing my little ticket booth with two roommates who otherwise would have been lynched by the *Lemons*: Lucas and Quasim. Even though it makes my place a bit crowded, the two of them stop the *Diggers* from taking over. *Diggers*? If you've ever lived below ground, you know what I'm talking about. Rough guys who feed on the city's waste. Me, they respect, because I provide them with the occasional trip to a better world. I wouldn't exactly call myself a Good Samaritan, but I don't make empty promises.

Lucas is a Coptic Christian. His wife's been dead for a long time. She got caught in the crossfire during some fight or the other in Syria and was hit by a ricochet shot. His son got killed that day, too. A real tragedy. Lucas doesn't dare venture out into the streets, rather spending his days and nights inside the ticket booth. I can't blame him. Like so many Copts, he's been through an Odyssey of violence. And when he and his brethren finally managed to escape from Syria in the Twenties, they ended up being bullied by the Arabs in the refugee shelters. Looking back, I guess I was lucky to be taken in by the nuns in the orphanage. They didn't suffer fools gladly, but at least you knew what to expect.

Quasim is less fearful than his buddy. He even goes out in the daytime now and then. He's a Yazidi. I like to rib him because of his religion, but I always keep it nice. I'm just joking, I swear. These guys are Zoroastrians. A faith older than Judaism, Quasim claims. Alas, not any more popular, I usually reply. During the exodus of the Yazidi from Syria even children had to lend a hand, toting their ancient tomes. A story, which I find touching. The little ones saved their peoples' holy scriptures from falling into the clutches of the so-called Islamic State, who saw the trek off with gunshots and grenades.

Living with the two of them can be a little trying at times. They simply don't stop arguing. As much as I understand that they have valid reasons to hate the *Lemons*, I don't want to come home to these bad vibrations after a long day of work. *Lemons* here, *Lemons* there. Blah, blah, blah. All the evils of this world, summed up in a book written in the seventh century. The *Lemons* will, step by step, turn Germany into a replica of Islamic State, the two of them insist. Lord have mercy with me, because their constant nagging wears me out. After thirty minutes I've had enough of their tirades. I hide my briefcase in a cavity under the floor-tiles, take off my Glock, and stuff a few units of coke into the pocket of my jacket. Then, I leave the ticket booth. My two roommates keep on bickering and don't even notice I'm gone. I need a bit of space right now. Alexanderplatz is my first destination.

When a train enters the station, I hop on the trailer hitch of the last car. On my way to Schillingstrasse I try to clear my head. Lights are gliding past, the shaft is filled with warm air. The smell of metal, sweat, and urine prevails. At Schillingstrasse station the train is searched for stowaways. The security guy's Alsatian starts barking at me, but five units of coke are enough to make his master happy. Dope, the only currency immune to inflation.

I emerge from the stuffy subway station and breathe in the fresh air that's blowing through the high-rise canyons of Alexanderplatz, where modern times have definitely arrived. Electro cars roll by almost without a sound, so that you don't hear them coming. It always takes me a while to get used to it. If I don't watch out, I'll get myself run over one of these days. Blessed be the roaring combustion engine, that's all I can say.

The young crowd can hardly wait for the night to start. The *Globals*, that's what the rich are called nowadays, have taken over the most coveted spots of this city and travel to the restaurants in chauffeured limos. Showing off their posh girlfriends, of course. On the weekends, the *Suburbians*, out for their weekly whiff of the scent of the great wide world, mingle with the party people. During the week they have to stick to a tight budget to be able to afford a night of pretending to belong. Waxing, peeling, tightening. Bodies buffed and smiles frozen in a temporary pretense of worldliness. Giving the friend in their company the stink eye, when he breaks out in a sweat once he realizes that he can't possibly compete with the trustafarians. Then follows the overwhelming fear, as it dawns on him that it might be the last time he's taking his arm candy for a stroll, before one of the *Globals* makes a go for her. And on the street corners homeless people bear silent witness to the luxury problems of others.

I go to a *Shower & Sleep Store*, rinse off the dirt and have my suit cleaned. These places also offer snooze cubicles for commuters, all lined up like honeycombs in a beehive. I call Anja and suggest dinner. She is her early twenties and a real looker. It takes her thirty minutes to get here by city train. When we say hello, I have to discipline myself not to be all over her straight away. We go to the *Hanging Gardens of Babylon*, a glassed in terraced café, soaring about 1000 feet up in the air. Premium seating, set on a steep angle. Private booths, too. Your view is drawn down like in a movie theater. The sunset over Grunewald replaces the silver screen, its luxury mansions white dots on the horizon. Most patrons ignore their attractive dates, staring through their data goggles instead. Processed reality. Meanwhile, the women, sunglasses on top of their hair, proceed to ogle the diamond display at the next table the old-fashioned way, which is using their own eyes. Quick, irritated looks are aimed at their not so affluent loser-boyfriends who can't buy them expensive bling. These women are absolutely convinced that life has dealt them a lousy hand. They've much more to offer in the looks department than the lucky ones do, right? Brave new world of post Capitalism.

Anja is skilled at small talk, while hiding her soul from me. Delicious pretender. In spite of the many times I've bedded her, she remains a stranger. Wrapped around each other, we make our way back to the *Shower & Sleep*, where I book a honeymoon box under the roof. Pure sex with a view of the star-studded sky. The old-fashioned way. That's how I like it. I hate entering through the back door. All this ass-fucking, which is getting more and more popular. I can very well do without it, thank you, Sir. The box has AC, shutting out the heat of the summer night. Still, we work up a sweat. I enjoy it as long as it lasts. There won't be anything left tomorrow.

4

After breakfast with Anja I call her a taxi, pay the driver in advance, kiss her good-bye, and promise to call her in the near future. "See you soon," she says when she gets into the car.

I send her away with a "Take care, little one."

Then I walk down Karl-Marx-Allee, until I reach Ghetto limits. The rising sun makes me blink. At checkpoint "Schilling" concrete steles and barriers made from barbed wire line a pot-hole riddled street. Armored cars are parked in front of the lowered stiles. Twitchy fingers on the triggers of their assault guns, the soldiers at the checkpoint don't let people pass any longer. Permit or no permit, it doesn't make any difference. The Ghetto has been sealed off. I stop in front of the International Movie Theater, wondering how to get home, when my phone rings. It's Natasha. She asks what I know of the assault.

"Assault?" I repeat.

"In Moabit," she explains. "Two suicide bombers with Kalashnikovs and explosive belts. Twenty-one people dead."

"I haven't listened to any news."

"They've attacked a school run by Jehovah's Witnesses."

"A school? Really? Bastards!"

"Thank God the guards were able to fend off these pigs. But then they started randomly firing at passers-by, before they finally blew themselves to kingdom come."

"Who's behind it?"

"We don't know yet. We're still busy scraping these guys off the street."

"I haven't heard anything about it. I swear."

"Where are you?" she asks.

"Checkpoint Schilling," I answer. "In front of the movie theater."

"Stay where you are. I'll come get you."

Fifteen minutes later Natasha arrives in her armored off-roader and I climb in.

"Did you have a chance to talk to the *Imam* yet?" she wants to know.

"Why? Do you think he ordered the attack?"

"He's not in the habit of making empty threats."

I nod, but I keep silent. I don't want her to know how great I feel. Last night's good sex still in my head and this morning's caffeine coursing through my veins. During the next hours the sun will travel across a perfectly blue sky. Considering the horrors that took place just a few miles from here, my happiness might seem quite inappropriate. I'm aware of it, after all I'm not a monster. I know that some people will never be able to again enjoy a wonderful day like this. And in many cases it's simply so damn unfair.

It's the first suicide attack we've had in years, I think. The situation was much tougher in the Twenties, volatile times, when the *Lemons* had the unfortunate habit to self-explode. Natasha seems to be convinced that the *Imam's* plotting a revival of this questionable tradition. It's an easy way to spread general fear and terror. Jihad's not just the name of some dim-witted thug who's taken a dislike to me, but also the time-honored battle cry of the *Lemons*.

Natasha studies me. "What are you doing here, by the way?"

"Getting fresh air," I reply.

She smiles. "A posh hooker again?"

I don't answer.

"Hauke, Hauke, you really need to grow up," she actually dares chastising me, as if she was my keeper. "Don't you ever feel like starting a family?"

"What about you?" I evade her question.

"When the time is right."

I look at Natasha. She has blue shadows under her eyes and seems to be sad, and there is more behind it than just the terrorist attack. She's carrying heavy baggage around with her, a dark presence, dimming the light of pride in her face. Since we've known each other she's been keeping a secret from me.

"We need to find out who sent this Salafist in the whorehouse to meet his maker," she says. "The *Imam* demands to know who pulled the strings."

"I know," I slowly say.

"What's your plan, then?"

I promise her to think of something, but she's not happy with my answer. I need something to offer to Natasha, or she'll keep pestering me. Goddamn ace of clubs. Poker cards ought to be made illegal. "I could pay a visit to the old *Tsar*." I'm groping for straws.

"The old *Tsar*? Dimitri Bashir?" My suggestion seems to surprise her.

I nod, yes. "He knows the Ghetto like the back of his hand."

"He's doing time in Sperenberg prior to being deported."

"I know. Could you drive me there?"

"Do you think it makes sense?"

"Why not? You'll never know without trying."

"Are you sure?"

"If there's something going down in the Ghetto, he'll know about it. He might be in jail, but he's still well connected.

Maybe he can tell us more about this business with the poker card."

"Okay." Natasha nods, yes, and starts the engine. "Let's grab a bite on the way. I haven't had breakfast yet."

"As long as you let me gaze into your beautiful eyes," I try to flirt.

Natasha gives a sardonic laugh. But I know that she feels flattered.

Sperenberg Penitentiary is located south of Berlin. Deep in the woods and cut off from the rest of the world, the *Lemons* cool their heels here, before military planes based at the nearby airport ship them back to their home countries. It's a maximum-security prison: double sally ports, steel gates, and very high concrete walls. The guards manning the towers have their grenade launchers pointed at the drive. Getting out of this place is not an easy feat. Natasha stays behind in the waiting area. She wants to keep in the background, because she hates confrontations with the Godfathers. Therefore, I make my way into the visitors' area by myself. Arms and legs shackled, Bashir is sitting behind a wall of glass. His complexion is as white as a sheet und his lips have a blueish tinge. Lung cancer in the final stage, I've been told. He doesn't seem to have many visitors any more and smiles, when he sees me. I would have never guessed that Bashir's face could register something like joy. He used to be a real hunk, but now his body is emaciated. A man whose fight will soon be over. A man at the end of his life.

"Hauke," he greets me, rubbing the dry skin on his face. He coughs. Then, he gets all teary-eyed and sentimental. "Do you remember how we last met on Strausberger? Back then, when I got married."

"To your third wife?"

"Yeah."

"I delivered a hefty amount of dope that day."

"So you did. My old lady must have popped half of it on her own."

"How's she doing these days?"

Bashir quickly performs a swiveling motion with his head, glancing at the guard standing next to him. "Beata." He turns back to me, whispering through the holes in the pane that separates us. "I cut up the ugly bitch's mug." For a moment his wrinkled face brightens with sadistic glee. Then, Bashir tells me about his ungrateful son who prevents his grandchildren from seeing him. He complains about the lousy conditions in jail and about the fact that Vasily—he calls the Chancellor by his first name—the rat has refused to grant him pardon. Solitary confinement either shuts people up or makes them loquacious. Bashir belongs to the second group. He just wants to see his grandson one last time, he says between bouts of coughing. And then the man actually breaks out in tears right in front of me. I don't feel sorry for him in the least. Because I'm thinking of all the people he has killed. The fifteen-year-old whose throat he cut in front of my very eyes, even though the kid was desperately pleading for his life. *Bitter old man, now you get what you've asked for*, I think. The little visitors' area wouldn't offer enough room to assemble all of the old *Tsar's* victims. I can see their ghosts, silently looming behind him. Patiently, they wait for him to take his last breath. And then he'll burn in hell.

"Maybe I can help you," I lie, my face a picture of sympathy as if I gave a shit about him. Even though it's nothing I'm proud of, I'd always do it again. "I can get you out of here," I offer. I don't hate myself for it.

Bashir's face lights up. Hope has been kindled.

"I really want to help you," I continue my dirty game.

"What do you want to know?"

"You play poker once in a while?" I ask.

The old *Tsar* frowns. "You crazy, man?"

"I was just thinking. What's the name of the game, where the ace of clubs is the second highest card?"

"What the hell are you talking about?"

"About the new player in the Ghetto who operates under the symbol of the crucifix."

"Crucifix?" Bashir seems to be confused. "You mean the kuffars from Nigeria? The pigs who finished off Boko Haram?" he shoots back. He then starts ranting about modern times in the Ghetto and how they still had a sense of honor in the old days. Rules. I let him carry on. The usual wisdom of the streets. "You know what these Soul Brothers are like," he rages. "One moment they cheer, the next they're yelping like lap dogs because their pretty little noses got broken. You wouldn't expect it from guys who're six feet tall and pumped up with anabolic steroids like a man bit by a snake."

I realize that Bashir doesn't know anything.

"You going already?" he asks confused when I get up.

"The tip with the Nigerians was good," I claim. Before I leave I assure him that he'll be out of there soon. Or see his grandson, at least. Dirty game.

I don't tell Natasha that the old *Tsar* is slowly losing it. "I need more time," I plead. But I feel her disappointment. As it's late already we spend the night at a motel on Berliner Ring autobahn. Natasha takes a separate room. When I try to kiss her forehead to tell her goodnight, she shrinks back, keeping me at arm's length like she always does.

5

Natasha drops me off at "Checkpoint Ring" east of the Ghetto. She shows her ID to the guards, ordering them to let me pass. Grudgingly, the uniforms comply. Through the fence, I watch Natasha leave. She backs up her car and drives away. I simply don't understand this woman. Does she see me as just a subordinate or does she have feelings for me? Soon I'm accosted by a few small-time dealers, wanting to buy dope. "Can't you see that I don't have my briefcase on me?" I wave them off, walk away, and continue on for another two blocks until I have reached the "Furuncle", which is where the bikers of Aryan Motorcircle gather. Eight bikes, guarded by a *Member* with a shotgun, are parked in front of the bar. His bandana is soaked with sweat and he's wearing his leather vest with badges even in the heat of the summer. His helmet sits next to the chair he has pushed onto the pavement. The club's insignia are steel helmets, adorned with white plumes. Once a week, the bikers parade down Jessnerstrasse. Fifty to sixty bikes in a narrow street, led by their blond president, who has a sculpted body and sports a winged helmet. Only the hammer is missing, otherwise he'd be mistaken for Thor from the comic books.

An old man with a twirled mustache is sitting on the stoop on front of the bar. He takes a sandwich from his pocket, eats a bite, and puts it away again. "You need to enter 222.wellwin.de," he addresses me. His head is turned in my direction, but he's staring into space. "Then you'll get activated," he expands on his tinfoil-hat theory. "Everything will be visible. And everybody. All that's hidden." *Crazy old geezer,* I think. However, he's not the only one around here whose synapses aren't wired properly. A woman grabs me by the arm. "Satan is a cheat!" the drugged-up human wreck warns me, eyes wide. I smile at her. Oh, how I love this crazy atmosphere in the ghetto. Madness, concentrated in an area of 2,000 acres. When I push open the door of *Furuncle*, the pounding of heavy metal music assaults my ears. Four booze-heads are sitting at the bar. A woman is gyrating around a pole. She's overweight and will never see forty again. In her tight latex outfit, she resembles an overstuffed sausage. Some members of the Aryan Motorcircle were already around when there still was an East Germany. Most of them, of course, need an oxygen tank by now or soil their diapers in some nursing home. And it's definitely not the music that made their bodies go to hell. Tom is at the bar, a whiskey bottle in front of him. He's in his early thirties and skinny and has been a *Prospect* for ten years now. A *Prospect* with the Aryans, that is. *Prospects* are the rookies, you know. Guys who still have to prove they're worthy and are bossed around by the regular gang members. Those of you who have served in the army know the hazing rituals of all-male communities. Tom will remain at the bottom rung of the ladder forever, I think, when I now look at him. A permanent rash covers his face. Each time I see him it blooms in yet another place. Today it's his nose, that's afflicted. He must be breaking some kind of record, not to have been promoted to *Member* for such a long time. But he can also be sure that the gang will never send him packing.

You simply gotta love working with *Omegas*. They're grateful for a pat on the shoulder and excellent providers of information. The physically weak make good listeners, I can tell you. They keep their eyes open and their ears to the ground. When Tom notices me, he gets up and shakes my hand. "Great to see you again." He really seems to be happy.

He's by no means an idiot. His eyes are alert and he's as sharp as a tack. It's simply beyond me why he puts up with all the abuse. He'd be able to get a Job in the City, where brains count more than brawn. He'd have a realistic chance to get out of the Ghetto, if he only wanted to. I'm wondering why he doesn't even try. Why he endures being humiliated by his so-called brothers. Maybe he just gets off on pain. We sit down at the bar and he pours me a whiskey. After we clink glasses, we both empty them in one gulp.

"How's it going?" I ask, pushing my last three units of coke in his direction.

"Oh, well," he slowly replies. "Not that great."

"What's wrong?"

"Thor hasn't shown up at the last parade."

The music drones out his soft voice. "You need to speak up," I tell him.

Tom leans over, until he almost touches my ear. "The filthy Arabs want to finish us up," he hisses.

"Yeah, yeah, so I've heard."

"Fucking fuckers."

"And what're you going to do about it?"

"Whaddaya think?"

"Get even?"

"Keep on dreaming. It's twenty of them against one of us."

"I know."

"What do you think, we can do?" he accusingly adds. "We're lucky if we don't lose our street."

"Yeah, I got it," I try to calm him.

Canned applause ends the performance of the overweight dancer. She comes over to the bar and has the bartender pour her a plum brandy. I look at Tom, twirling my empty glass in my hand. I need to find out if he knows anything about the ace-of-clubs-crucifix murders. "You guys are not on a crusade, you know what I mean?" I ask, all the while carefully studying him from the corner of my eye.

Tom bristles. "Why do you say something like this?"

"Why do I say what?"

"The thing about the crusade."

"No special reason," I claim.

Tom bangs a tattoo on the bar with his storm lighter. "Must have something to do with the sun spots, that's why everyone's suddenly going nuts."

When I smile at him, he doesn't meet my eyes. He always avoids eye contact. Like we were animals and he was a subordinate male. "What, if the tables could be turned and the Arabs would be grabbed by the balls for a change?" I insist.

A pensive nod from Tom. "I wouldn't mind."

"These guys will finish them up, you think?"

"What *guys*?"

"You know who I'm talking about."

"What do I know?"

"What they're saying on the street."

"About who? The roof-runner?"

I slam my hand down on the bar. "Then you do know what's going on," I blurt.

Tom points at the badges on his vest. "Being a *Prospect* doesn't mean you're blind," he declares.

I bend closer to him. "Speak up! Who's behind it? Who're the Arabs scared of?"

Tom refills his whiskey glass. "It's just talk." A dismissive wave with his hand.

I put my arm around his shoulder, pulling his upper body closer to me. "Tell me," I urge him.

"Abdul," Tom starts, struggling to shake off my arm.

"So what?"

"Abdul who lives on Revaler, I sometimes have a chat with him. He's told me something," Tom explains.

"You're chatting with an Arab?"

"Yes, why not? Not all of them are bastards." Tom lowers his head until it almost touches the bar. "Abdul's scared shitless," he continues. "He's told me he was just dragging his ass down Revaler early one morning, when he saw this... hell, I don't know..."

"What did he see?" I don't let go.

"A weird shadow." Tom swallows. "What's the right word? A dark figure, running across the rooftops."

"Dark figure?" I wonder aloud, lifting my brows. "There's plenty of those around here," I add.

"No, no, not one of the usual motherfuckers," Tom protests.

"Meaning what?"

"Okay... the way he moved... light on his feet. And the way he was dressed."

I shake my head. "The way he was *dressed*? I don't know what you're talking about."

Something seems to distract Tom, because he turns his head in the direction of the window as if having a kind of premonition. Next, the pane explodes. The staccato of at least two submachine guns. Projectiles ricochet around the room. The barman returns the fire straight away, blindly spraying the street with bullets. The two booze-heads take a dive behind the bar, followed by the pole dancer. Tom takes cover behind the pool table. Squashed cigarette butts at eye level, I remain on the floor in the middle of the cross-fire. I remember a drive-by shooting I witnessed while standing in the middle of a street. Fifteen years have since passed. I had better reflexes back then. And I had my Glock on me. Now, my guns are at home in the ticket booth. I can't do anything but hurl pretzel sticks. Damn. Twenty or thirty seconds later the show's over. I lift my head. Pieces of glass have gotten into my mouth and are stuck to my face. I pick myself up, spit them out and dust off my suit. Tom casts a nervous look at the bartender, who's reloading his shotgun. Armed *Members* come thundering down from upstairs. I follow one of the heavily inked men outside. The guard at the entrance is down and covered in blood. The man has caught it in the chest two or three times. His breathing is labored. The old geezer is still on the stoop and grins as if everything was just fine and dandy. The woman Satanist is on the sidewalk, all bloodied up. She must have smacked her head against the pavers. I can't see any gunshot wounds. I want to help her get up, but when she starts screaming like a banshee and tries to hit me, I leave her be. The attackers have vanished into thin air. They must have driven their car around the block and into the next side street. Tom and two other bikers carry their dying comrade into the clubhouse. "Who did that?" I ask him.

"T'wasn't the roof-runner, right?" Tom replies, before the bullet-riddled door falls shut behind him.

I turn around. The street is quiet now. In the building across, there is someone at the window. When the woman realizes that I can see her behind the pane, she shrinks back. I look down Frankfurter Allee, where "Checkpoint Ring" is. The soldiers have retreated behind the wall of sandbags. They won't move a finger to help. They don't care what's happening inside the Ghetto.

6

Gray and drab. Submerged into the dust of the city. The monk's habit resembles a patchwork rug. A black wooden crucifix aimlessly dangles around the neck of the killer. He tiptoes across the rooftops, almost without causing a sound. Driven by revenge, even barbed wire can't stop him. The man pulls back his hood, produces a pair of bolt cutters, and carefully severs one strand after the other, until the barrier of spiked wires is down. Twenty-four years are a long time—but the score has to be settled. The crime can't go unpunished, no matter how long it takes. With his bare hands he pushes aside the barbed wire. The cuts in his skin only serve to remind him of the suffering of the murder victims. Drops of blood hit the ground, but he doesn't care. He takes a leap onto the roof of the neighboring building, flexes his legs, and silently rolls over.

Gazing down on Strausberger Platz, the guard squashes his cigarette on the balustrade, not realizing that someone is approaching him from behind. The last thing he sees is the dried out basin of the waterspout fountain, before the garrote closes around his neck, cutting off his air-supply. The killer remains faceless up to his final moment and is nothing but a gust of hot breath, caressing his neck. Before the guard takes his last breath himself, he thinks of the prostitute he was planning to marry. The shadow releases the dead body from his strangling embrace and lets it sink to the ground. After he has relieved the guard of his silenced gun, he walks through the open access to the roof and climbs the stairs. The high-rise at Frankfurter Tor is made of glass, offering a 360°-view of the city. A man sits in front of the TV screen, only dressed in his underwear and stoned from three lines of coke. On his lap there is a bag of potato chips, which he stuffs into his mouth without tasting them. Slowly masticating but not enjoying the spicy flavor of paprika. The porn flick continues, and the chips make crunchy noises between his teeth. When he notices something from the corner of his eyes, he lifts his head. A dark figure is approaching at a hypnotically slow pace. Always moving and moving, as if drawn closer by an inner force.

"I've been expecting you," the man says, not the least surprised. "My whole life I've been preparing myself for this moment. Now, the time seems to have come." He motions the intruder to come closer. "You might as well get it over with, bastard."

The stranger nods. He takes out his cudgel and keeps on walking toward his victim. Twenty-four years, and nothing has been forgotten. Nothing has been forgiven.

Drones are circling in the sky above F'hain. Natasha sounds pretty nervous on the phone. A big city honcho has announced his visit. There are elections coming up and, as all of you are surely aware of, this prospect makes politicians suddenly become very energetic. A foray into the Ghetto is usually part of the program, under police protection, of course. Drones and sometimes even a police helicopter or two. Dozens of snipers on the rooftops. This way a seemingly cleared spot in the center of anarchy can be presented to the public to make the shuttled-in TV teams believe that there has been real progress in the fight against poverty and extremism. You all know how this bullshit works. In this case the itinerary doesn't even include the Ghetto proper, but only the puffer zone around East Side Gallery, where *Lemons* and Germans interface. Rows and rows of outlet stores, with the "Halal Arena" nestling in their middle. The hall doesn't only host Islamist bingo nights but also the *Lemon's* most major wrestling event ever. Here, the *Muslim Terminator*—a three-hundred-pound behemoth—stomps the *Christian Satan*—a hundred-and-twenty-pound scrawny kid—into the ground every other day in an eternal loop. People just love it, even though the outcome is predictable. Maybe it's because the *Christian Satan* has the unfortunate habit of bombarding the heroic defender of the half-moon with every creative insult known to man. No idea. As today's opening act the *Imam* is scheduled to preach to his flock. Next to him in the ring, he has a special guest, no other than the politician who's trying to get re-elected: Helmut von Schlotow, mayor of our venerable city by trade. I wouldn't want to be seen dead in this place, if not for Natasha's insistence that the fight might provide me with a once-in-a-lifetime chance to have a little chat with the *Imam*. She tells me there's an agreement with Schlotow to allow me inside the *Imam's* private lounge as part of the mayor's delegation. My first reaction is to adamantly refuse. I'm still extremely hung over. Also, I don't seem to be able to shake off dark premonitions of trouble, gathering on the horizon. Nightmares, as disturbing as a painting by Hieronymus Bosch. *The Last Judgement,* maybe. Gruesome punishment. Death and destruction. Natasha doesn't give up until I declare myself beaten and trudge along to the arena.

The "Private Security Area" begins right behind Oberbaum-brücke. Sheriffs in black uniforms guard the entrance to the amusement zone. They are headquartered in a watchtower in front of East Side Gallery. Unlike the fence that surrounds this party area, these guys in black really present an obstacle. Everyone knows that they have no qualms to open fire on unauthorized intruders. Now and then the victims of these disciplinary steps can be seen floating in the River Spree. The bodies usually drift all the way down to Jannowitzbrücke, where they're finally fished out of the water. Just in time, lest the view of bloated corpses might affect the *Globals'* marriage proposals, often made during leisurely evening strolls along the riverbank.

"Why does he always wear sunglasses?" I ask Natasha, while the *Imam* basks in the adoration of his followers. Our seats are in the upmost box, far away from the general *Lemon* population. Although the word "box" evokes images of luxury, painfully absent from the shabby interior of the arena.

"There's something wrong with his eyes," she explains. "They say that he's almost blind."

"Blind? Really? He's moving around pretty nimbly for a blind guy."

We both study the tall man in his off-white caftan. He's protected by at least one bodyguard like usual. Ali Bansuri, the most powerful man in the Ghetto. 62 years of age, eight wives, 43 children. One of his daughters serves as a representative in the Bundestag, the German Parliament. Two of his wives are still girls, fourteen and fifteen years old. Bansuri means flute. And he eagerly sticks his flute into every orifice he can find. His face looks friendly. Just imagine your generic grandfather. While Bansuri enjoys the adulations of his fan club, Natasha rolls her eyes. I know how much she resents him. Bansuri is a preacher but, most of all, he's a businessman. After a short introduction, followed by some quotes and meaningless formal greetings, he asks the members of his flock for donations to his *Islamic Relief Organization*. Many mosques are in a deplorable state, he complains. People are avoiding the houses of prayer, all the while committing sins in the privacy of their homes. The spectators in the lower tiers start to booh. They're exclusively male and black-haired, most of them sporting full beards. The veiled women crowd in the upper level. Their robes are black. What this arena sorely lacks is some color, I think. Next, the *Imam* lists the games of chance the faithful are allowed to engage in.

Bingo is *halal*—okay.

Laughing while playing bingo, though, is *haram*—not okay.

Roulette is *haram*.

Wheel of fortune is *haram*.

One-armed bandits are *haram*.

Card games are *haram*.

These *Lemons* really know how to make the place rock. The *Imam* has the crowd hanging on to his lips. Almost foaming at the mouth, he's screaming into the mike, dictating the rules of life and agitating against the infidels. But his emotional eruption of outrage is nothing but cool calculation. A routine performance. A controlled display of fervor, as if he were an actor on stage. He continues to whip up the masses, until his bearded puppets are seething with hatred. Bansuri claims that it's the infidels who keep Muslims in poverty. During his diatribe von Schlotow just stands there, shifting from one foot to the other. The *Imam* lets the rage of the audience wash over the ashen-faced politician for a while, before he deigns to relieve the poor guy of his misery. If relief is the right word. Because Bansuri then announces that the mayor is planning to convert to Islam. No idea if it's true. Maybe it's just a PR gag. There are too many fake converts around, to whom joining a religion is nothing more than signing the contract for a new job. You know how politicians tick. The honest Abes among them are usually left behind in the dust or ignored by the average citizen. Charisma is the cousin of vanity. Which is the stuff, blinkers are made of. Schlotow seems to play along. Many *Lemons* are registered voters. Gullible souls, just ripe for picking. And he seems to need all the votes he can get. He also doesn't really run a risk. Because the speech in its full length is only broadcast in the *Lemon* neighborhoods. The Germans in the nicer parts of the city have their own media. Customized political campaigns, truth made to fit for every target-group. Just tell them what they want to hear. And most journalists know the name of the game. But maybe there are fifty righteous men left in this town, I remind myself of the truism one of the nuns used to quote when I needed to be disciplined.

Soon, Natasha and I are both bored to tears. After a while she opens the top button of her blouse. She likes my eyes to roam across her cleavage. "Last night, Ramsan Alchanov was killed at Frankfurter Tor," she says, as if stating the obvious.

"Alchanov," I repeat absently, because I'm busy admiring her tits. "A Chechen, right?" I ask, just to make sure.

"Yeah," She replies. "Someone stuck an ace of clubs between his fingers," she elaborates.

The mention of the poker card makes me sit up. "Have you been to the scene?"

Natasha shakes her head, no. "You know that the Chechens would never allow it."

"Just asking," I say.

"They sent a photo to the LKA."

"A portrait of the late Ramsan?" I take a guess.

She nods again.

"It doesn't mean a thing," I point out. "Maybe the photo has been tampered with."

"Maybe."

I suddenly have a brainstorm. "There might be more than one killer. Or a copycat."

"No, I don't think so. I'm convinced that we're dealing with one perp only."

"We shouldn't get too fixed on the poker card."

"You know my view on this ace-of-clubs angle."

"If it's really the same guy, it raises one important question, I think."

"Shoot."

"What did the two victims have in common? For what possible reason should anyone kill the Arab manager of a whorehouse and a Chechen porn producer?"

Natasha buttons up her blouse. "That's exactly what you're going to find out."

I shake my head, no. "I'm peddling drugs. You're the investigator."

"You have the right contacts inside the Ghetto."

"They're called customers."

"That's why you are my informer. Do you honestly believe that these guys would bare their souls to a LKA detective?"

I wave her off. "They won't trust a snitch like me either."

"But you're very convincing."

"Convincing?" I repeat.

"Right," she replies with a downright lovely smile.

"And how exactly will I convince Bansuri to talk to me?"

"With the aid of two pounds of coke," she dryly answers, holding out a plastic bag to me.

I shake my head, because I can't believe what I'm hearing. "You're carting around this much dope in a cheap bag?"

"Why not?"

"Well, the packaging is a tad lacking in style, I should say."

"Here, where Orient and Occident meet"—the *Imam* has meanwhile worked himself up into a lather—"the one and only true faith will win its final victory." His words are followed by the theme music of the *Muslim Terminator*. The spectators jump off their seats and start clapping frenetically. The women in their segregated upper levels are screaming like banshees and wave signs, offering themselves for marriage to this humanoid monster. I lean back and close my eyes. The cheering turns into white noise, as I doze off.

Natasha wakes me when the spectacle is over. The *Imam* declares the *Muslim Terminator* the winner. The loser is wrapped in a bloody sheet and carried from the arena. The crowd's had its fun. We leave the box before everyone else gets up. Natasha points out his one weak spot to me to prepare me for my meeting with the *Imam*. It's Khalid, his firstborn, 46, unmarried, no children. Enjoying life to the hilt in his penthouse above Alexanderplatz. Much to his old man's chagrin, he jets around the world and parties with fancy hookers. He's the steady thorn in the *Imam's* flesh. I know Khalid well. He's my best customer. I sell him every unit I can spare. Khalid pays well. Even a Pusher doesn't mind a little revenue on the side, you know.

When we make our way down the steps of the arena, Natasha's treating me like a schoolboy, lecturing me on how to proceed. I just hate it when she's acting superior like this. After all I'm the one who lives in the Ghetto, while she shacks up with some rich dude in X'berg. What does she have to teach me about life? With a pat on the shoulder she sends me on my way down the corridor to the locker rooms, where I'm frisked by the mayor's security guy. Then, it's the turn of the *Imam's* Salafist guard to pat me down. Glock and briefcase have to stay behind.

The home-team's locker room is a sorry sight to behold. The *Imam* is seated on a simple chair right next to the Jacuzzi. Von Schlotow's on a little stool beside the man of the cloth.

Bansuri is lecturing the mayor about the plight of his brethren in faith here in Berlin. The crime in the Ghetto, the access controls, the fortifications. So many of his people were languishing in the city's jails. The new madrassa in Zehlendorf will remedy the situation, Schlotow promises. Bansuri nods happily and seems to be placated. Still, he steers the conversation to the murders in the Ghetto. The crucifix was carried into Jerusalem once, he says. It brought death and destruction over the Muslims, he points out. Then, he takes a deep breath and drops the bombshell: Even though already two dead relatives of his have been garnished with aces of clubs, the *Imam* has not seen it fit to inform the LKA of these crimes. You don't usually discuss internal affairs like this with infidels, he adds, full of his own importance.

Schlotow seems to be helpless in the face of the *Imam's* arrogance. Before he leaves, he kisses the Quran proffered by Bansuri and walks out of the locker room. When the mayor is gone, the *Imam* motions me closer. "The messenger of Satan, the scum of the earth," is his flattering way to greet me. "What does he have for me?" He addresses me in the third person, his voice a hypnotic monotone. When I approach, he issues a staccato of clicking noises. Like a bat getting its bearings with the help of ultrasonic waves, he seems to use echo as a means of orientation. This way, he can probably guesstimate my position. A bodyguard hands him the plastic bag containing the coke. Bansuri sticks his hand inside and fondles the little pouches with a satisfied nod. "Five minutes," he says.

The shades stop me from seeing Bansuri's eyes. My first instinct is to check, whether the man is really blind. But the older one of the two bodyguards is watching me like a hawk. I'd rather not find out what he'd do if he reads one of my movements as an insult. "I need to compliment you," I lie through my teeth. "They say you've beheaded six Chechens with your own hand. What an act of courage."

The *Imam* eagerly nods.

"However, I ask myself," I continue, "how the blade has met its mark."

Bansuri laughs. "The first cut doesn't need to be the last one," he hints at the way the execution took place. "It's enough if the fourth of fifth strike kills. I wanted them to know how much I've enjoyed their screams. And I wanted to smell their sweat of fear, when my blow smashed their shoulders and the scimitar dug into their hips. Allah in his wisdom has honed my remaining senses. A blind man perceives the things that count. He can hear the melody of the world, unadulterated by treacherous eyes." A beatific smile on his lips, the *Imam* starts softly chanting verses from the Quran.

"There were two more murders before the one of the great Yussuf Bansuri?" I ask.

"Tarek and Abdul, my dear brothers, have died in an ambush carried out by the crusader," the *Imam* complains. "May Allah punish him," he adds with a hiss.

"When did it start?" I want to know.

The *Imam* takes his time. My straight question seems to annoy him. It obviously makes him feel uncomfortable to discuss a family matter with an infidel like me. He looks in my direction as if to discern what to make of me. "A little over two weeks ago we found Tarek in his tea house with his skull shattered," he lets me know. "The shisha was still in his hand. I swear, when I get my hands on this crusader I'll have him tortured. For weeks. Months. Inshallah!"

"Yesterday Ramsan Alchanov was murdered," I inform him. "An ace of clubs was found with his body."

The *Imam* flinches as if struck by lightning. "The crusader kills like a coward," he tries to mask his deep confusion with a platitude. "Crusaders or Jews, it's all the same to me. They poison the minds of our young men, seduce our women, and rob us of our culture. If this Christian isn't apprehended soon, I'll take the fight out of the Ghetto, inshallah," he grimly declares.

Bansuri didn't know anything about the murder of the Chechen, this much is clear. He seems to be shocked, even. Now, I'm really confused. Why should he mind so much, that a Chechen's been killed? Might he see a connection to the series of murders, which are news for Natasha and me?

With a flick of his hand Bansuri motions to one of his bodyguards to see me out. The audience is over.

8

The Copt's getting more and more paranoid. Lucas and Quasim continue to encourage each in their hatred of the *Lemons*. Now, they even badger me to get them some fertilizer to build a bomb. It had to lead to problems eventually that they do nothing but hang out in an underground ticket booth on a subway platform brooding, without ever seeing the sun. Lucas is right of course when he says that the *Lemons* have been persecuting the Copts for centuries, suppressing them and destroying their culture. But you can't dwell on the past forever. Life has to go on. Again and again I try to talk sense to him and to cheer him up. Quasim is no real help in this. Most of the time he just sits on the sofa, doesn't say a word, and numbly stares into space. These bad vibrations are simply more than I can take. I'd love to just walk away and leave the two of them to their own devices. Maybe I'd better look for another place to stay in the Ghetto. There might not be any apartments available, but the tunnels under the city offer many hideaways up for grabs.

I'm not sure what to do. For some reason Lucas has grown to me. Maybe it's because he's an honest and decent guy, qualities I'd like to claim for myself. Therefore, it hurts twice as much that he's blaming me and my drug-dealing for the moral decay all around. He accuses me of infesting the Ghetto with dope. The fact that it's my only option if I want to make a living, doesn't count. Even though he also benefits from my business, as I often grumble. The money for meat in the refrigerator had to come from somewhere, right? However, I'd never say so to his face. Not, as long as he's down like this. I don't want to find him with his wrists cut when I come home. When I casually mention that the *Imam* plans to build yet another madrassa, this time in Zehlendorf, Lucas sits up. I just let him vent his anger against the *Lemons*. Quasim will join the chorus, meaning that the two of them will leave me alone.

Anja's getting more and more demanding when I take her out. Her blatant materialism exhausts me. All these endless shopping orgies in the fancy fashion stores along Kurfürstendamm. Fortunately, these places now have lounges for stressed-out guys that even serve free drinks. One day Anja points out a diamond necklace to me and tells me, how much she likes it. *Hint, hint.* She smiles at me. Sex is very involved that night. She pleases me with her mouth for the first time ever. She must really want these baubles. Which reminds me to severely cut down on the free dope samples and to raise the price for Khalid. Priorities. I don't run a charity organization and I'm not a good Samaritan either. Once I've paid the admission fee to her innermost sanctuary, the demands will hopefully stop for the next few months.

Natasha calls me a couple of times a day, demanding regular reports on my progress. I can't do anything but ask her for patience. She's told me that the DNA on the poker cards they've found is useless. The worn-out cards have gone through too many hands. Fortunately, there hasn't been another attack since the assault on the school. But we're living on borrowed time. The storm will break loose eventually. We both know it.

I fill some vials with neurotoxin, arm my briefcase, and pocket four spare magazines for my Uzi. The Glock's set back on escalation, step one. Tonight I'll lay in wait. If this roof-runner shows his face, I'll catch him red-handed.

9

The muezzin's just calling folks to five o'clock tea, when I make my way up to the roof of one of the Stalin buildings on Frankfurter Allee. I watch life unfold on the street, lined with car wrecks and garbage heaps, until dusk starts to settle. Wannabees, performing wheelies on their pimped-up motorbikes. Men, beating their wives with belts without worrying about witnesses. Boys, getting a whipping from their fathers. Nothing out of the ordinary. Patiently, I wait until the sun is low on the horizon. Veiled women, six children in tow, scurry home through the twilight to seek shelter inside their apartments until the next morning. It's not just criminals who live here. But after sunset only gangbangers populate the buildings' doorways. As electricity gets shut off in the Ghetto, the streets are quickly growing dark. The coughing bouts of sick children fill the night. Does life on other planets look like this, too? Do people who live many light years away also congregate in their places of worship to march in circles around the fragment of a meteorite, lost in trance?

The next morning I'm yawning so much that I almost unhinge my yaw. Besides a few junkies and some teens who stole out of their rooms in the middle of the night nobody has shown up on the roof. I walk down the stairs and leave the Stalin building. Today, I'm not in the mood to return to the subway tunnel.

"Hey, Hauke, yalla," a homeless guy addresses me. He's sitting on the stoop of a porticoed doorway. It's Umit, one of the worst boozers I've ever met. He's close to fifty, his face bloated after thousands of alcoholic binges. Coarse skin, the bags under his eyes could be mistaken for balconies. He's virtually evaporating booze. His ripe odor keeps the Sharia police away, I guess. Stink to fend off the Islamist guardians of virtue. Life can be really strange sometimes. Umit always carefully combs back his curls. He gels them almost lovingly. He must be very proud of them.

"You've fucked with Jihad, yalla," he slurs.

Jihad. I've totally forgotten about this little punk. We've left off at escalation step one, if I remember right. "How do you know?" I ask.

"Yalla, Jihad's sounding off, he's gonna ice de Pusher, yalla," Umit replies.

"So?"

"Jihad's a big guy on de Warsaw, yalla. He's mighty pissed off, you know."

"So what? What do I care?" I hand Umit two units of coke. "Guys like him are always pissed off about something."

"You'd better watch your back, kuffar," his drinking buddy chimes in.

Umit gives a hoarse laugh. Then he crosses his hands behind his neck and turns his face into the rising sun. It looks like he's planning to enjoy the warm rays of the celestial body with the help of a bottle of vodka. A perfect day for a homeless dude. His pants are encrusted with last weeks' urine. Once you've reached a certain alcohol level you lose control over your bladder. Before I leave, I give the two of them a casual two-finger salute.

It would be an option to turn around and take a detour to Petersburger Strasse to spend a more or less relaxing day at the Volkspark. But somehow the challenge awaiting me on the Warsaw beckons me. I switch over to the median, where I can hide between the trunks of the plane trees in case of emergency. This early in the morning the street is deserted. The inhabitants of the wooden shacks, set up between the burned-out wrecks of cars, haven't risen yet. Just a few devout believers are hurrying to morning prayer. I unlock my Glock, open the buckle, and put my finger on the trigger button of the needle in my case. A child excitedly takes off into the building at the kebab store where I had my run-in with Jihad. The kid must have recognized me. I close my eyes and take a deep breath, when adrenaline floods my body. Nervousness dampens my hands. I feel a pulse beating in my neck and my knees start to tremble. Ultimate bliss. Still in his undershirt and a Mac 10 in hand, Jihad comes running out into the street. He seems to mean business. A bare twenty yards in front of me he stops, waving his submachine gun, and starts heaping abuse on many generations of my ancestors. The idea behind it must be to retrace my entire family tree all the way back to Adam and Eve. "Fucker! Fucker! Fucker!" he screams. The impact of my rubber round has left a perfectly round angry spot right on his forehead. I vault behind a plane tree just in time, before he begins manically emptying the magazine of his submachine gun. Hatred cast in lead drills its way into the bark of the tree. But there's no magazine in this world that will hold enough rounds to satisfy a retarded out-of-control Ghetto teen. When I hear an empty click, I leave my shelter and point my Glock at him while he's still busy reloading. My first shot zooms past his left ear by inches.

"You missed, kuffar," he gloats, brandishing his newly loaded gun.

"I wouldn't be so sure about that," I reply. My next shot hits his shoulder. Escalation step two. Jihad drops his gun at once and starts screaming like a man possessed. His friends rush to his aid, firearms in the ready. Enough time for me to once again take refuge behind my wooden barrier. A plane tree can withstand a lot of bullets. The attackers don't dare come closer. Armed to the teeth and still quaking in their boots. Respect is something you have to work hard to get.

The persistent honking of a car horn distracts everyone. The shooting stops. I peer out from behind my cover. A low-slung Beemer has arrived. I watch the irate teens begin a heated debate with the driver. The car's windows are darkened, but I can make out the license plate: "Babo 2". It's Cem, the right hand of Selim, the Turkish Godfather. After a while the kids reluctantly turn away from the car, even though they don't stop cursing me. Jihad, who's meanwhile convulsing on the ground with pain, is hauled from the street into the kebab store. Two of the guys remain standing in the doorway. They give me the stink eye and aim globs of saliva at the pavement. Cem rolls down his side window and motions me over to the car. "What do you think you're doing, Pusher?" he asks me, shaking his head.

"Just a little early-morning exercise," I inform him.

"This block *Imam's* block, yalla!" I hear Jihad's shrill voice from inside the kebab store. He seems to be in a lot of pain. "*Babo's* not big boss here, yalla."

"Get in, brother," Cem orders. He won't take no for an answer.

I slide onto the Beemer's passenger seat. Cem steps on the gas. The teens storm out into the street, threatening me with their guns—but they don't open fire.

Cem shakes his head. "Aren't you a little too old to play these games, brother?"

"Why?" I deposit ten units of coke on the dashboard. "There's nothing but a good tussle to make a guy feel young again." I grin.

"You're one weird bastard."

I study Cem from the passenger seat. "Why am I sitting here?"

"Selim wants to talk to you."

"So? Really? How come the *Babo*'s suddenly interested in me?"

"He'll tell you himself."

Cem switches gears and makes a turn into Revaler Strasse. He's about my age and I like him. He looks at things with the eyes of a businessman, just as I do. Without emotions, purely rational. A rare quality among the hot-blooded *Lemons*. They say he even went to university for a few years as a young man. Physics. But eventually he must have found out that there are easier and faster ways to make money. Cem was already working for Halim, the current *Babo*'s father. He was recruited for his brains and also because he's extremely loyal.

"Are you still fooling around with your three steps of escalation?" he wants to know.

I smile instead of an answer.

"This is fucking baby stuff," he chides me. "There are more important things in life."

"What could be more important than having fun?"

Cem pulls down the corners of his mouth. "There will be a war," he sagely predicts.

"So?" I ask, pretending to be bored. "That's the way things are in the Ghetto, right?"

"Just wait and see," he warns me. "I'm starting to get very worried here. If the Templar keeps on killing people, we'll have a real problem."

"The Templar?" I repeat, feigning ignorance. "You're buying this bullshit, too?" I emit a groan. "Jesus. A stupid ace of clubs and everyone's going crazy."

"Allah have mercy on us." After kissing his hand, Cem reverently touches a bobblehead figurine shaped like a whirling dervish.

"Why do you *Lemons* always think that everyone's out to conspire against you?" I rib Cem. "Templars have died out a long time ago."

"I know the system behind it, brother. I know what the Templar's up to. The murders... he's trying to sic us Muslims on each other." Cem turns to face me and gives me a reproachful look as if the whole thing was my fault.

"Do you think that I...?"

Cem waves me off. "No sweat, Pusher. No sweat. I don't bear a grudge against you, brother." When he smiles at me, I breathe a sigh of relief. There won't be a little detour to a back alley, where a firing squad's lying in wait.

Cem drives me to *Club Berghain*, where Selim resides. The hall has been totally refurbished and they still play electronic music here, like they did over twenty years ago. Retro rules supreme, take my word for it. Cem leads me to the office behind the dance floor. Selim is at a desk in a room, filled with cigarette smoke. He angrily rubs his forehead. The ashtray is overflowing with butts and there is an open file folder in front of him. He must be doing his book keeping, if this is the right word to use in his line of business. Selim is only in his late twenties. Already at an early age he had to take over from his father, who's been confined to a wheelchair since suffering a stroke. One alcoholic binge too many, rumor goes. Selim's men are in awe him in spite of his baby face. Or maybe just because of it. A seemingly harmless non-threatening person who brutally knifes his opponents is bound to leave a much deeper impression than your typical stony-faced thug. Selim has long stepped out of the shadow of his overpowering and tyrannical father, who did his best to made him feel like a loser. He greets me with a smile. "Hey, look at the maggot we've got here," he says. "The Pusher, what a surprise," he adds.

"Long time, no see," I reply.

"How'd you get here?"

"Ask Cem," I answer.

Selim laughs.

Cem gives me a shove from behind. "Show some respect, Pusher," he admonishes me.

Selim motions to Cem to keep quiet. "I like this kuffar. Really. You can't trust him, but his coke is still the best."

I nod, walking up to the desk to open my briefcase. But Cem yanks it out of my hand. "You know the rules," he hisses, lifting the lid himself. He takes out three pouches of coke and puts them on the desk.

"You gotta leave me one pack," I protest.

Selim nods. "Put one back in the case," he orders Cem.

Cem complies, shuts the case, and returns it to me.

"Why did you have me brought here?" I ask the *Babo*.

"You know the answer, *Pooosher*," Selim drawls.

"Because of this... Templar guy?"

"This fucking Christian pig," Selim confirms.

"How does it concern you?" I wonder aloud. "So far he's left your people alone."

"Oh, he did, didn't he?" the Babo rages. "And what, may I ask you, will the *Imam* have to say if the Templar continues to spare us?"

"No idea. You tell me."

"What do you think? That we're behind the whole thing, right?"

"Now, aren't you taking things a bit too far?"

"Do you really believe so?"

"I was in the 'Halal Arena'," I reply. "The *Imam* was cursing the Christians and the Jews, not the Turks."

Selim slams his fist on the table. "Bullshit!" he yells. "You know very well that asshole Bansuri spouts lies as soon as he opens his mouth. Do you really think he believes that the *Potatoes* did it?"

"Why shouldn't he?"

"Bullshit!"

"And you really don't have anything to do with it?" I enquire.

"Are you crazy?"

"Some dead Arabs and a Chechen stiff as treat. Isn't this the stuff your wet dreams are made of?"

Selim shakes his head, smiling. "Don't get me wrong. I don't mind some of Bansuri's bastards being dead. And that Ramsan's bought it doesn't hurt either. The little rat was a real nuisance, 'cause he suspected me and Bakh..." Selim bites down on his lip. He casts an anxious glance at Cem, who relaxes in a chair, smokes a joint, and doesn't seem to listen.

"What did he suspect?" I probe.

"None of your business, Pusher." Selim evades my question. "It's private."

The door opens to admit a woman, who's muttering curses under her breath. When she sees me, she quickly pulls her scarf over her head. After this concession to dress code she starts laying it on with a vengeance. "You're ignoring me!" she accuses the *Babo*, wildly waving her hands about. "You're treating me like I'm nothing to you. And at night you... you never touch me."

"Piss off, Aisha. Dammit," Selim hisses. "This is a business meeting."

"I will leave you!" Aisha threatens. "I will go away."

"Yeah?" the Babo replies. "You must have forgotten what happens to unfaithful wives."

Aisha breaks out in tears. "I'll go live with the *Potatoes*. Outside the Ghetto."

"And what do you plan to use for money?" Selim sneers.

"I'll clean houses or wipe the wrinkly asses of old *Potatoes*, I don't care. Everything's better than having to be with you."

"Do you think it was my idea?" Selim hollers. "Do you honestly think I would have married a slut like you if I had a choice?"

"You... you...," Aisha sobs. Cem steps up to her from behind, puts his arm around her shoulder, and leads her out of the room.

"It was my father's wish! Go and complain to him!" Selim calls after her angrily.

"I'll leave you," Aisha threatens again. Cem closes the door behind her.

Selim's shaking his head. "I don't believe it."

"Trouble?"

"Never mind."

"I'm glad to hear so."

"This won't leave this room. Got it?" Selim warns me.

"Who should I tell it to?" I reply, feigning boredom.

"Promise?"

"Why did you send for me?" I ignore his question.

"First I need to know if this will stay between you and me," he insists.

"What's supposed to stay between you and me?" I pretend not to know what he's talking about.

Selim smiles. "So we have an understanding."

"Now, spit it out. What did you want to tell me?"

Selim jams the tip of a dart into the desktop as hard as he can. "If the Templar carries on with his plan, there'll be a disaster," he whispers.

"What plan?"

"I didn't see a connection between the murders at first. There was no reason to. But today, at sunrise, someone left a photo on the doorstep of my club. Cem found it."

"What was on the photo?"

"I now know who'll be the next victim."

He has my full attention. "What the hell are you talking about?"

"Allah have mercy with us, if we fail to stop the Templar." Selim produces a photo from the top drawer of his desk and studies it. "The choice of situations in which people agree to have their picture taken will always remain a mystery to me," he pensively adds. "They don't seem to waste a thought on the possibility that they might later be held accountable. That's how proud they are of what they did. Bunch of idiots!"

He passes me the photo. I have to force myself to stay calm, because I don't want Selim to know how excited I am. Therefore, I try just to take a casual glance at the picture, as if I had more important things on my mind. It's not easy, I can tell you. Quite difficult, actually. I almost lose control over my features. No wonder, considering what's on the photo. I hold my breath. A group of fighters's mugging for the camera with some kind of desert as a backdrop. Wide grins on their faces, they're waving their Kalashnikovs in the air and seem to be having a great time. In the sand at their feet I can make out a number of butchered people. Their clothes are bloody. Their heads have been severed from their bodies. Limbs twisted in unnatural angles, they present a picture of desolation. The men in the group seem to be overjoyed about the massacre they must have just committed.

I recognize:

Tarek Bansuri.

Abdul Bansuri.

Yussuf Bansuri.

Ramsan Alchanov.

The four victims of the roof-runner, or Templar as the Turks call him.

Next to Ramsan Alchanov there's a man wearing a balaclava. I can't tell who it is. His hand holds a butcher knife, smeared with blood. And in the right-hand corner of the picture, proudly displaying the flag of the Islamic State, a sixth man is posing for the camera. My throat constricts. Even though the guy on the photo has aged a lot, I still see at first glance that it is Ali Bansuri. The venerable *Imam* himself, triumphantly striking a pose behind his beheaded victims, flanked by his brethren in faith. Without shades, but already sporting his long beard, he exudes middle-aged virility.

10

When I was a boy I went to collect Burgundy snails one day. It had just rained and they came crawling out from under the hedges, which made it easy to pluck them off the paved path. I delivered them to the woman who made a business of selling them. When I handed over my plastic bag full of snails, she gave me ten Euros—our currency until fifteen years ago, just in case you've forgotten. Anyway, it was a lot of money for a child in those days. The woman dumped the snails with their fellows waiting in crates in the yard, ready to be shipped off. For a long time I just stood, watching the snails, squashed shell against shell inside these wooden crates, trying to wiggle their slimy bodies through the slats. Hundreds of them, squeezing their heads through the gaps, while blindly searching around with their feelers. All they wanted was to escape from their wooden prisons. But it was hopeless, of course. Their calcium shells held them back, shelter and restraint in one.

The sad picture of the writhing bodies stayed with me for many years. Snails might not be the smartest creatures under the sun, but I still felt sorry for them. Exactly because their resources are so limited as compared to ours. I'm sure they never wanted to end up in somebody's cooking pot. I didn't bring the woman any more snails. The next half-full bag I just emptied into a ditch.

Like the snail, whose escape is prevented by its ornate calcium cell, something is also holding me down inside the Ghetto. It is a force that remains beyond my grasp. I'd have a chance to find happiness in the world out there. Maybe with Natasha even. But I can't get the 'hood out of my system. As if the black soul of an utterly corrupted being had me in its clutches.

I'm just sitting here without knowing how I've spent the last couple of hours. Maybe it would be a good idea to start taking my meds again. Could Natasha get me a refill, I wonder? Phone in hand, I'm totally at a loss. Have I called her already to tell her that the *Imam* is next on the roof-runner's list? His motive is revenge, directed against the Caliphate's soldiers. This much is clear by now. The roof-runner wants someone to pay for the murders, committed by the Islamic State. Have I told Natasha that the Ghetto will drown in a deluge of blood? Have I told her anything of importance at all? Told her what I feel? I'm talking and talking without really saying anything. My phone rings. I stare at the screen. It's Khalid, the *Imam's* son. He invites me over to his penthouse on Alexanderplatz. He needs me to bring enough coke, to get his party going again. I pick myself up. Leaving my guns behind, I surf the next subway to Schillingstrasse. When I get there, I bribe the sheriffs, leave the station, and let the doorman in the foyer of Condominium 1 phone Khalid. I'm cleared to step into the elevator and take it up to the top floor. Humongous bodyguards frisk me and allow me access to their charge. The smell inside the penthouse is ripe. The pungent odor of vomit is wafting over from one of the bathrooms. I'd rather not know what it looks like inside. Stuffy used up air assaults my nostrils, the curtains are drawn. On the sofas, a few unclad fancy hookers are sleeping it off.

I push open the door leading to the outside and cross the roof garden belonging to the penthouse. Bikinis are floating in the Jacuzzi, empty champagne bottles adorn the tiles. Cigarettes have been squashed in the left-over drumsticks on the buffet.

Khalid's standing at the balustrade, looking out over P'Berg. He's wearing a white sheet like a toga. When he notices me, he tilts his head to the side. "You're late, Pusher," he says, bored.

"Party's over, right?"

"No, my friend. The party's only getting started now."

I put the pouch containing two hundred units on a table. Khalid smiles. "New fuel... very nice."

"You know where your father is?" I ask.

Khalid turns away from me, bends over the balustrade, and aims a glob of mucus into the abyss. "I can make my snot fly seven-hundred feet now," he gloats.

"If it doesn't hit a window before," I point out.

"Right." Khalid gives a pensive nod. "You don't get to choose your family," he adds.

I come a step closer. "I wouldn't know, I don't have one."

"Maybe... maybe it's better sometimes."

"No, it's not. I swear."

"What's wrong?" he asks.

"Your father is in danger."

"So?" A derisive laugh from Khalid. "What's new?"

"It's serious this time. Very serious."

Khalid nods. "So what?"

"You'd better warn him."

"Warn him? Of what? Who would be dumb enough to try to kill him?"

"And if the other guy happens to be a step ahead?"

Khalid waves me off. "My father's a survival artist," he dismisses my concern. He walks over to the buffet, plucks a cigarette butt from a drumstick, and holds it to the flame of an oil lamp to light it.

I follow him out, deeper into the roof garden. "How much do you know about your father's past?" I ask him.

Khalid sits on a bench under a palm tree. "What you want to know? How he used to work me over with a belt buckle, maybe?"

"Has he fought with the Islamic State?"

"Islamic State?" Khalid repeats. My mention of the terrorist organization seems to confuse him. "Do they still exist?"

"No idea. What do I care? I'm talking about twenty years ago."

"Twenty years? That's a long time. A hell of a long time." Khalid drags on his cigarette, drawing the smoke deep into his lungs. "Al-Qaeda, ISIS, Boko Haram. My father had his dirty fingers in every pie."

"He still had his eyesight back then?"

Khalid nods. "Eyes like an eagle, he prided himself. Yes. But Allah in his wisdom has struck the bastard with an illness. All he can see now is shadows. The shadows of his victims."

"What happened to his eyes?"

"It began about ten years ago. Suddenly, his retina started to come off. He slowly, but surely, lost his eyesight during the following years." Khalid tosses the cigarette butt to the ground and steps on it. "Allah must have heard my prayers." He gives a sarcastic laugh.

"Did he take part in the massacres?" I want to know.

"What do you think?"

"What did he tell you?"

"Of course he was involved. The guy wasn't squeamish. Torture, executions, you name it. He used to boast that he even served as minister of education in ISIS for a couple of weeks."

"Your father's in danger."

"Who the fuck cares?"

"He's your father, after all."

"Let's call him the sperm donor."

"He might be next on the list."

"List?" Khalid frowns. "What list are you talking about?"

"The list, the roof-runner's currently working his way down."

"Roof-runner? You're talking about the crusader who's butchering Salafists?"

"Exactly the one."

Khalid laughs dismissively. "You know what? I'm simply not interested. The killing won't stop anyway. The Ghetto… everything seems so far away to me." He points at the ventilation system of the high-rise behind him. "Somewhere beyond this mountain of iron the abyss begins. The scum'll devour itself. Inshallah."

"If there's a war it'll spill over eventually," I warn him.

"Why should there be a war? One imam dies, the next one follows."

"There's a crucifix involved."

Khalid's face darkens. "Selim has already mentioned it."

"Selim?" I wonder aloud. "Are you in contact with the *Babo*?"

Khalid nods, yes. "I invite him over to my parties now and then. He always brings his boyfriend."

"Boyfriend?"

"You didn't know?"

"Is he gay or what?"

"You really had no idea?"

"No. How could I?"

"I thought you're so well informed, Pusher."

"Well, I guess I'm not."

Khalid runs a hand through his gelled hair. "Selim thinks that my father might blame him for the murders."

"I know."

Khalid smiles. "But Selim doesn't really worry about himself or his own safety. The fag's scared because of someone else. The idiot's hell over heels in love."

"In love?"

"You would never guess with a killer like him."

"What's his boyfriend's name?"

"You're really clueless?" Khalid can't believe it.

"Who is it? Do I know him?"

"You've heard of Bekhan, I suppose," Khalid declares with a wide grin.

"What? Bekhan Bashir? The young *Tsar*?" I can hardly trust my ears.

"Looks like it."

I wipe my hand across my mouth. "Impossible! The *Babo* and the *Tsar* a gay couple? You're joking, right?"

Khalid smiles. "A real whammy, right? But it's the honest truth."

"It can't be…," I slowly mumble. "Could it be a motive?"

"You used to be more in on it, Pusher," Khalid chides me.

My phone rings. "Excuse me," I say.

"Why?"

"I need to take this." I retrace my steps through the roof garden and push open the sliding door.

"What's wrong with you, Pusher?" Khalid calls after me.

I glance at the screen. It's Quasim. Where does he have my number from? When I take the call, I can hear him whimper. He says I need to come home at once. Then, he hangs up. Something terrible must have happened.

11

At "Checkpoint Schilling" armored personnel carriers have taken position. Hundreds of soldiers are preparing for action. The national guard and the militias also have been put on alert. Police officers are discussing strategy with the storm troop commanders, coordinating last-minute details with the help of maps. Disciplinary action against the Ghetto seems to be on the agenda. From time to time the government launches tactical sorties to teach the *Lemons* a lesson on who's boss in this city. A blunt weapon in the authorities' fight against the clans, but effective when it comes to winning votes. And, as you already know, we have elections coming up. Might Schlotow still be bristling after the dressing-down he received from the *Imam*, I muse. Another explanation could be that a video of the event in the "Halal Arena" has been leaked to the outside. Never mind, I need to hurry up before all entrances to the Ghetto are sealed. My permit convinces the soldier at the stile that I'm legitimate. After a nervous glance in the direction of his assembled comrades he quickly waves me through.

I make my way to the subway tunnel via the basement of the derelict building. Once there, I let a train pass and then walk along the tracks to Samariterstrasse station.

Something's very wrong there. Books and brochures have been yanked from the shelves inside the kiosk and tossed onto the tracks. Outside the ticket booth, my clothes are strewn about all over the place. What's happened here? I jump onto the platform, sneak up to the kiosk, and peer through the window. Nobody. I scuttle over to the ticket booth and listen at the door. Nothing. I enter my lair on tiptoes and look around. Someone has found my hiding place under the tiles. My briefcase is on the sofa, its secret compartment open. The Uzi's been removed. I reach for the submachine gun to check if it's loaded, and sniff at the muzzle. The gun hasn't been fired. Next, I hear someone whimper. Gun raised, I walk over to the living area. The scene in front of my eyes sends a cold shiver down my spine and I lower my gun. Quasim is on the bed, covered in blood. His hand holds the Glock.

"Hauke," he moans when he sees me.

I sit on the side of the bed, put down the Uzi, and support Quasim's head. The bedcover is literally saturated with blood. In his despair, Quasim has used a belt as a tourniquet around his thigh. His leg artery must have taken a hit. And it's not the only gunshot wound he has. His shirt is full of blood. Buttons pop, when I rip it open. Shocked, I see the bullet hole in the left side of his chest. Dark-red blood is oozing out of a deep crater. The slug must have gotten stuck close to his heart. There's no way to save him.

"Hauke," Quasim groans.

"Who did this?" I ask.

"They took Lucas away with them."

"Lucas?"

"They… beat him up and hauled him along."

"Who the hell did this to you?" I want to know.

Quasim's head slumps and he closes his eyes.

"Who were these bastards?" I insist, leaning over him, and grab his hand.

Quasim gives my hand a weak squeeze. "You need to kill him," he implores me.

"Who?" I ask, desperate. "Who did this?", I repeat, my forehead pressed to his.

Slowly, Quasim opens his eyes. "The *Imam*," he barely manages to whisper. "You have to…" Quasim takes his last breath. Two more shuddering gasps for air, and then he's gone.

I close his eyes and pull the blanket over his head.

Lucas. I say his name as if echoing Quasim's voice. "I need to save him," I repeat to myself. Over and over. My hands are clenched to fists. I stare at the blood-soaked sheet for a while, trying to get my thoughts straight. Therefore, I hardly hear my phone ring. It's Natasha. She warns me of an imminent purge and advises to lay low. I wordlessly end the call. When she calls again, I let it go to voicemail. After a while I shake off my apathy and reach for my Glock and my Uzi. Then, I pick up the four magazines from the floor and tuck them under my belt. The submachine gun goes back into the briefcase.

The door to the bathroom is open, the light is on. When I come closer I notice an odd coat on the sink. It seems to consist of nothing but patches. On the floor next to the commode there's a wooden crucifix. I search the coat pockets: bolt cutters and a garrote. A pouch tied to a loop of rope contains two poker cards. Both of them aces of clubs. The coat belongs to the crusader. The Christian. The murderer. It's not really a coat actually but, with its hood, looks more like a monk's habit. Old and threadbare. Is this the getup of a Templar? Might the *Babo* be right, after all? I look around, pricking up my ears. Is the killer still somewhere nearby? A high-pitched screeching fills my ears like an attack of tinnitus. My head's pounding. Without thinking, I stuff habit, poker cards, and bolt cutters into my briefcase. They're important evidence for Natasha. In the sink I notice a cudgel and a gun. A Walther PPK with a silencer. The magazine is full. I pocket both weapons. When I leave the ticket booth I see a picture someone's taped to the mirrored pane. Who? It's the photo of a painting, showing a group of haloed men. I don't understand what it's supposed to tell me. I peel the photo off the pane and look at the back.

Icon of the 21 Martyrs.
Never forget the men who have died for the Holy Cause. Remember the sacrifice, made by the 21 Coptic Christians.

Martyrs. Sacrifice. I stuff the photo into my pocket. Glock raised, I leave the ticket booth. I hear a train coming. A woman in the back car gives me a scared look. It only lasts the bat of an eyelash, then she's gone. For a while I just stand there like frozen. One hand holds the Glock, the other one my briefcase with Uzi and evidence. Thousands of unorganized thoughts are zinging around my brain, competing for attention. I can't get my head around what I've just seen. I'm unable to put it into perspective. I touch the Glock to my forehead, as if the cold steel of the gun's muzzle could soothe me. There are moments in life when everything boils down to the things that matter. The decision becomes clear. You're stripped of all pretense. Cleansed of guilt. You feel that everything you've done and thought so far doesn't make a difference. All the while knowing, who you really are and what your job is. The cacophony of thoughts gradually dies down until there is only one left. The one that gives your life a purpose.

An eye for an eye and a tooth for a tooth.

I have to avenge Quasim and to free Lucas from his prison. And nothing can stop me. For this is the only reason I have been put on the face of this earth. My head has never been clearer before, maybe I have never been happier. I shudder and look at the Glock in my hand. Sweat is pouring off my face and trickles down my back. Every fiber of my body is like a live wire. It feels simply great.

12

Without ever stopping, I hurry through the labyrinth of sewers. I know these underground pathways like the back of my hand, because I use them a lot. Markings on the walls help me not to get lost. Now and then I hear gunshots, echoing off the walls of the tunnels. The attack of the storm troopers seems to be in full swing. The purge of the Ghetto has begun. Darkness starts to set in when I leave the sewers, quietly making my way along the dam of the abandoned tracks of the circular train. My destination looms right in front of me: the mosque on Landsberger Allee, where the stockyard used to be. I can see the four minarets and the ramparts of the adjoining palace. The compound is surrounded by a high wall, but I know a secret access through a sewage pipe. I labor through the underbrush, without noticing the sting nettles that abound here. Spiders scurry across my face. Mosquitos are closing in. I don't begrudge them their bloody feast. When I reach the mouth of the sewage pipe, I use my bolt cutters to snap the locks securing the grid. I crawl through the pipe, pushing my briefcase ahead of me. Eventually the passage widens. A shaft is leading up. I climb the rungs, carefully open the lid of the manhole, and peer out. I'm in the middle of a large courtyard. Pillars adorn the impressive buildings. Filigree patterns grace the archways. This is the *Imam's* palace. A rectangular water basin, oblong flower beds, neatly manicured hedges. The epitome of luxury. When I look around, there's not a soul to be seen. Maybe the *Imam's* henchmen and their charge have taken shelter in his private chambers, lest the soldiers try to arrest him. The ramparts of the central tower show me the way to his quarters.

Two guards flank the double doors that lead to a side wing. The Walther's silencer comes in handy. I neutralize the men without making a sound. The path is clear. Like a thief, I tiptoe down the corridors until I reach an atrium with a waterspout fountain. I smell frankincense. The fragrance of *The Arabian Nights.* I make quick work of one more security man and stow away his corpse in a bathroom: gold-plated faucets, marble slabs on the floor.

I get to a pillared hall, its walls decorated with calligraphic symbols, when I'm startled by a voice calling out to me. I have been discovered. I duck behind a pillar. The guard fires at me, but his shot just bounces off the column. I hear more voices, as others hurry to his aid. Now, it's time for the Uzi. I empty a magazine, spraying the four guards with bullets, while they are rushing at me. They never stand a chance. I quickly reload and shoot at the two men who are now coming down the stairs. My movements are fluid, my actions those of a robot. Pierced by a number of slugs, the men tumble down the steps and slump on the floor. They're both dead. Ignoring the first guard, who's still firing at me, I run up the stairs to the first floor, my opponent stubbornly on my heels. I kick open a door, look around the bedroom behind it, cross an antechamber, and gingerly open a door to the hall, where I stop. The guard thinks I'm still in the other room and turns his back to me. Plop. Plop. The Walther ends his life, barely making a sound.

While I climb floor after floor, a TV feature about the *Imam* comes to mind. His lair was located in the fifth floor of the fortified tower, he then boasted to the beautiful blonde female reporter.

When I push open a door I end up in a windowless room. I lower my gun. The view in front of me sends a shiver down my spine. Arranged around a calligraphic ornament on the floor, spears have been anchored in holes drilled into the marble slabs. I hold my breath. There are heads impaled on these spears. Skulls and hair are glistening as if coated with a layer of wax. Little name plaques nailed to the shafts of the spears list the names of their owners. I recognize the six Chechens, the *Imam's* first victims after he seized power. But there are other faces I've never seen before. The features of the dead lose their distinctive marks with time like those of mummies. Some of the heads date from decades ago. My guess is that it must be more than sixty of them altogether. A chronicle of the *Imam's* murderous career. The story of a deplorable life, as told by the heads of the dead. I walk along the row of heads, only looking up now and then. When I finally stop, I have to swallow. This is the view I've been afraid of all along. My hope evaporates that I can still make it in time. For the row ends with the head of Lucas. I stop for a while, lost in thought as if I was praying. Then, I pull the head off the spear, put it on a chair, and carefully wrap it in a blanket. I want to spare him this last indignity.

Lucas was the roof-runner, the killer of the Salafists. This much is clear. He wanted to avenge the 21 martyrs. The photo of the group must have fallen into his hands somehow. The one with the *Imam* and the other ruthless murderers, posing in an unknown desert. He's the one who killed the Chechen and the Arabs. However, he failed to fool a blind man of the cloth. Ali Bansuri, your time has come to pay for all the evil you did. I'll be the hand, Lucas doesn't have any longer. I'll be his tool. I take the habit from my briefcase and put it on. It fits like a glove. After I have donned the hood, I reach for the Glock. The case and the other gun I leave behind. When I hear noises from the bedroom, I check the magazine of the pistol. The dum-dum bullet is waiting right on top. Step number three. Much too easy for a bastard like him.

13

An old man is in front of a fireplace, hastily tearing out sheets from a file folder and tossing them into the flames. Even though he is blind, he easily finds the next file on his desk. The old man seems to try to destroy evidence before the police has a chance to search his palace. Suddenly, he stops. "Nadim?" he asks, confused. "Is this you?" The man produces a sequence of short clicking noises with his tongue while turning his head in all directions. Startled, he drops the file and walks back to the fireplace, where he pulls a poker from the stand and holds it in front of him in an attempt to protect himself. "Who are you?" he asks in the general direction of the sound, feeling around with his poker. "What do you want?" The old man is convinced that the intruder must be a stranger. He keeps on waving his poker until it gets caught on something. The poker is yanked from his hand. "Nadim!" the old man calls out. "Get help! Quick!" He nimbly hurries around the desk and pulls open the top drawer. A sudden pain makes him slump to the floor. A blow to his side takes his breath away. He needs a while to recover. The old man gathers all his strength and starts crawling across the carpet. Try to get to the scimitar on the wall, he tells himself. A gunshot. White-hot pain makes him cry out. When he presses his hand to his thigh, he feels warm blood, seeping out between his fingers. Where the muscle used to be, there now is a deep crater. "I didn't do anything," he moans.

There is no answer.

Another three yards. That's the distance across the carpet the old man has to cover, before he can pick himself up somehow and make a grab for the weapon. Possible, even with a gunshot wound as serious as his.

A sound makes him stop. Someone has taken the saber from its bracket on the wall. The stranger has been quicker. The blade hisses through the air a few times, before it grazes his neck. Almost tenderly, the cold metal strokes the old man's skin.

"Do you know who you're dealing with?" someone suddenly whispers into his ear. It's a deep and unfamiliar voice. "Do you know who's going to chop your head off now?"

The stranger must be very close. The old man turns over to his back, flailing his arms.

Derisive laughter fills the room. "Do you know my name?"

"Listen, we can find a solution. How much do you want?"

Again, derisive laughter.

"I'm rich enough to give you anything you desire," the old man promises.

"Dead men don't need money." The stranger does not seem to be interested in a deal.

"What?"

No answer.

"Who… who are you?"

"You remember the men you and your comrades marched across the sand of the desert?"

"Desert? What…?"

"You had a great time. There was not a trace of sympathy, when you looked at your beheaded victims."

"Oh, that's the reason?" Slowly, it dawns on the old man why the stranger is here. He pictures the faces of the murder victims. One after the other. Engraved in his memory like the last impressions on his retinas before he grew blind. "Times were different back then. This… I… It was Ramsan, who… it was his idea," he tries to save his neck.

"You're not blind any longer," the stranger's voice triumphantly states. "You remember what your eyes have seen. Those who

90

have been killed by you and the henchmen of Islamic State. All the way back, twenty-four years ago."

"It wasn't me who swung the butcher's knife." The old man continues to refuse responsibility.

"Your time is up."

"I…" the old man starts, but then swallows because his mouth is dry.

"Hold your neck straight, this way it will be easier for you."

"I'm not ready to die yet!" the old man protests, trying to protect his face with his arms.

"You made your choice," the stranger replies.

"Nooooo!", the old man screams. Pain makes him flinch. He tries to get his bearings and doesn't understand what is going on. In his confusion he wants to touch his head, but it seems to be much too far away for his hands. Hands? What hands?

"Your time has come," the stranger announces.

"Allah, have mercy with me," the old man whimpers. Blood is running down his face. He hears the steel swishing through the air again, making contact with the marble floor. The old man doesn't feel pain. He doesn't feel anything at all. What is this supposed to mean? Has the coward missed him? Yeah, this must be the reason. The saber has been clumsily swung, the blow hasn't hit home. I've won out again, the old man gloats. They'll never get me. Allah's light will shine on me forever.

Next, the old man's head is rolling away to the side, while the rest of his body remains still, the wide grin on his face frozen for eternity.

14

A corpse without a head is not a pretty thing to behold. Even if it's the corpse of Ali Bansuri. His mirrored shades have remained firmly in place and he still seems to be grinning. As if triumphant even in death. I pull a poker card from the cloth pouch, dangling from my habit on a piece of rope. Then, I wedge the card between the fingers of one of the severed hands. There's one ace of clubs left in the pouch. It's meant for the sixth man on the photo. The executioner with the butcher's knife and the balaclava covering his face.

"Filthy son of a bitch!" I hear someone scream behind me. When I turn around, one of Bansuri's bodyguards rushes into the room and loses no time to open fire. My hand is holding the scimitar, my Glock isn't ready to shoot, I've no way to defend myself. Two slugs hit my shoulder and chest and I slump to the floor. The guard starts kicking me, maddened with rage. I can't really blame him. He's out of a job now. And odds are that he won't be getting a new one so fast. Who wants to hire a bodyguard who failed to protect his boss?

"Son of a dirty whore," he continues cursing me. He raises his gun and points it at my face. A shot rings out—but I'm still around to hear it. The bodyguard's face freezes. Blood comes pouring from of his nose and he collapses. In the door I notice a woman wearing a burka. She lowers her gun and slowly approaches. Then, she lifts her veil. It's Natasha. Sweet, wonderful Natasha. She kneels next to me and takes my hand. "Hold on," she says.

Everything is fine, Natasha. I finished my job. There's nothing left for me to do. I feel my strength seeping away. I'm unable to speak. My head sags forward and everything starts turning black. I don't even manage to keep down my lunch. Now, I'll have to go on my last journey on an empty stomach. Even dead people digest food, I've read. Also, their hair and nails continue to grow. Shit. Who came up with this bright idea?

What's awaiting me on the other side? God or some other higher being? Or just nothingness? Honestly, my friends, I couldn't even begin to guess.

Epilogue

LKA Berlin, central division, Headquarters at Oberbaum-brücke, X'berg. Two days later.

Detective Natasha Lieberknecht runs her hands across her tired eyes and takes a deep breath.

Then, she knocks on her superior's door, and when she's told to come in she enters the office on the top floor of the high-rise. Her eyes wander past her supervisor to the Ghetto beyond River Spree. From three hundred feet up crime is just a vague notion.

"Congratulations, you did a great job," Commissioner Richard Volkner greets her from behind his desk.

"Congratulations?" Natasha repeats.

"I had my doubts at first, but your *Operation Martyr* turned out to be a tremendous success. The *Imam* is dead and his spawn won't come crawling out of the Ghetto so fast."

"I don't really feel like celebrating."

"Our punitive measure also enabled us to track down quite a number of arms depots," the Commissioner continues, ignoring her protests. "The clans have been dealt a devastating blow. It'll take months for them to regroup."

"And then we'll be back to square one," the Detective points out with a frustrated sigh.

"So what?" the Commissioner retorts. "We've bought time."

"But there were so many casualties…"

"Yeah," the Commissioner agrees. "But don't forget how many lives we've saved in the end."

"… and also keep in mind the victims in my team," the Detective pensively adds.

"Well." The Commissioner looks up. "Will he make it? Your snitch, I mean."

"He's got a sturdy constitution."

"I really hope that he'll pull through. Very much. Maybe we'll need to use him again in the future," he continues, his voice reflecting cold calculation. "You shouldn't let things get so close to you," he tries to cheer up his subordinate.

"I try my best not to."

The Commissioner studies her carefully. "You look a bit pale."

"It was a tough week."

"You know what Franz's told me? That you actually sat at this guy's bedside the whole goddamn night!"

The Detective nods. "Yeah, that's right."

"Why?"

"I..." She falters.

The Commissioner frowns. "You'd better not get... well, you know what I mean."

"No, no," the Detective is quick to assure him. "It was all strictly professional."

"Right." The Commissioner takes a file from a stack and starts turning the pages. He shakes his head. "Hauke Jablonski. A schizophrenic madman."

"Strictly speaking he isn't schizophrenic," the Detective protests.

"Say that again?"

"He's suffering from an imprinting identity disorder."

"I still can't believe that he actually decapitated Bansuri. And he chopped off his hands, too?"

"He didn't stop at that. He also impaled the *Imam's* head on a poker. Who can tell what he really saw? Hallucinations are part of his illness."

"I don't understand how he even got access to Bansuri. The *Imam* was surrounded by bodyguards."

"Hauke neutralized half a dozen of security men."

"Jesus! This psychopath seems to be impossible to control."

"Only if you don't catch him in the phases between his episodes. That's when he's susceptible to imprinting."

"Imprinting," the director repeats. "That was the plan, at least. Even though I don't really know how it works," he admits. "You once told me that another word for his illness was histrionic personality disorder."

"This term is obsolete."

"But there's always a dominant personality, right? The man you see on a regular basis, I mean. Is the Pusher his—how shall I put it—*original* personality?"

"It's his constant personality, remaining after each episode."

"As compared to the other personalities that are obliterated during these episodes?"

"That's how the doctor explained it to me."

"Well, never mind. Your experiment... pardon the expression... was extremely successful. As risky as it might have been to take him off his meds, the strategy was highly innovative. To imprint him on two of the Salafists' victims. Simply brilliant. What were their names again?"

"Lucas and Quasim."

"You leaked their stories to him?"

"Hauke always hung out in the abandoned kiosk in Samariterstrasse subway station, leafing through the old cartoons and magazines that were gathering dust there. Thus, it wasn't difficult to smuggle in the reports about the ISIS massacres that got him interested. Some photos of the people murdered and their bios did the job."

"And he... well... *identified* with them?"

"The official term for it is imprinting, I think. They became integral parts of his personality."

"And when did he see this group photo of Al Bansuri and the other ISIS thugs we had received, courtesy of the Federal Intelligence Service?"

"Four days after his medication was discontinued. When the imprinting phase was over, I thought that the time was right to steer Hauke's hatred toward the killers of Lucas and Quasim. In the hope that he'd kill the *Imam* and the other Salafists to avenge them."

"Brilliant. I can only repeat myself."

"However, the angle with the crucifix on the playing cards wasn't part of the plan. No idea why Hauke planted them at the scenes. The situation would have almost gotten out of control."

The Commissioner turns the pages of the informer's file. "Well, here in the medical test reports it says that Herr Jablonski is a character given to extremes. *All or nothing*, is the way they put it."

"Hauke invests all he has into everything he does," the Detective explains. "I tried to talk him out of the business with the poker cards. I even took him along to see the dead whorehouse manager. But the experience doesn't seem to have gotten through to the rest of Hauke's identities. I should have... the whole thing is... it's really..."

"Natasha!" the Commissioner emphatically cuts in. "Stop looking so miserable. There are camera teams waiting in the lobby downstairs. The reporters want to interview you. You're the city's new hero."

"Hero? You must be joking! I've betrayed almost everything I've ever believed in. All my ideals. When I started to work here..."

"Nonsense! The Ghetto scum has been taught a lesson. The Chancellor wants to see me later... and... you, too, of course. Wear a nice skirt suit with lapels wide enough for the decoration."

"Decoration?"

"What else? Don't tell me you didn't know."

"And Hauke?" the Detective quietly asks.

"What about him?" the Commissioner is surprised. "The public can't ever know about him. He's an informer..."

"... who deserves an award."

"A drug dealer?" the Commissioner asks, not trusting his ears. "Natasha, Natasha, what are you talking about? What we need is heroic figures like you. Not some seedy pusher character. People want idols they can look up to. Who inspire them. Are you going to freshen up a little now?"

"I don't think it's appropriate..."

"A hint of blush and some of this new-fangled skin spray my wife's recently started to use," the Commissioner interrupts her. "Take my word for it, nobody has use for a broken hero."

Heartfelt thanks to all who have supported me during the publishing process of this novella, especially my wonderful crew: Ingo, Michael, Sylvia, Ilona, Janet, and my dear mother. In memoriam to my dear father, Fritz Krepinsky.

I also send a huge thank you to my Lovelybooks rounds! It's so great sharing with you!

In memoriam Franziska Pigulla, who has recited my novel *Spreeblut* with so much passion.

Best regards to everyone at *Goodies*, *Westberlin*, *Oslo*, *Kala*, and all the other Berlin cafés, where I hung out to write. SomaFM Dronezone is and will always be the best musical background when in my own (rental) home.

Like always I'm tremendously grateful to my readers, who have awarded me, an independent writer, with their trust. If you have questions or suggestions, please write to: info@nichtdiewelt.de.

Take care and stay safe!
Karsten Krepinsky

www.theworldbehindthewindow.com

The author

Karsten Krepinsky is a German author and lives in Berlin. He holds a PhD in biology. When not working for a start-up company in the field of neurosciences, his passion is to write mystery, sci-fi, and horror novels. A great source of inspiration to Karsten is the vibrant city of Berlin.

The translator

Karin Dufner, holder of an M.A. in American literature, has been working as a translator of fiction since 1989, seeing herself as a wanderer between the English and the German language. Her bibliography encompasses around 400 titles. Her ivory tower is located in the Düsseldorf area, Germany.

The cover designer

Ingo Krepinsky is co-founder and manager of the Bremen, Germany based design agency Die Typonauten. He studied communication design at the University of the Arts Bremen and the University of Applied Sciences and Arts Hannover. He has won several design contests such as *iF communication design award*, *The German Design Award* (nominated) or *Stiftung Buchkunst* (best designed books). The design performance and font work of Die Typonauten are consistently presented in international journals. The foundry was selected as German independent type foundry for *Typography, Referenced – A Comprehensive Visual Guide to the Language, History, and Practice of Typography*, a publication of Rockport Publishers.